I0843164

His Paradise

Natoshia Baer

Copyright 2024 Natoshia Baer All rights reserved

The characters and events portrayed in this book are fictitious. Any similarity to real persons

No part of this book may be reproduced

ISBN Paperback: 979-8-9865940-9-5

ISBN Ebook: 979-8-9865940-8-8

Cover design- Avery Designs

Formatting- Danielle Lynn Books

Printed in the United States of America

Another book, Papaw. I wish you were here to see it. But I know you're with me, because you're my sunshine.

Contents

Content Warnings

This book contains mature content that is NOT suitable for anyone under the age of eighteen. This is a dark romance, which will carry some dark themes. Those themes include the following.

- Domestic Violence (not from the love interest but from her ex.)

- Torture

- Violence, including weapons

- Near-death of a loved one

- Threat of Sexual Assault

- Kidnapping

- A mother separated from her child (but the child is perfectly safe at home the entire time.)

- Fighting, action, and occasional gore

Resources

Resources for anyone who needs them. While I hope none of you ever will, I've included them here just in case. Stay safe, and know that you are important.

If you or anyone you know is experiencing domestic abuse, you're not alone. The National Domestic Violence Hotline (NDVH) is a 24-hour confidential service for survivors, victims, and those affected by domestic violence. Advocates are available at **1-800-799-SAFE (7233)** and through online chatting at

The following resource has been copied directly from the website:

<u>Clare's Law</u>, also known as the Domestic Violence Disclosure Scheme (DVDS) is a police policy giving people the right to know if their current or ex-partner has any previous history of violence or abuse.

The scheme is named after Clare Wood, who was murdered by her abusive ex-boyfriend in 2009. It was formally rolled out in England

and Wales in 2014, following the landmark campaign led by Clare's father Michael Brown. **Under Clare's Law, you have the right to:-**Make an application to the police requesting information about your current or ex-partner because you are worried they may have been abusive in the past and believe they may pose a risk to you in future. Request information from the police about the current or ex-partner of a close friend, neighbour or family member, because you are concerned that they might be at risk of domestic abuse in future.**This is called the 'right to ask.'** You have a right to ask the police no matter if your enquiry relates to a heterosexual or same-sex relationship, as long as you are aged 16 or older. You also have the right to ask about a partner regardless of your (or your neighbour, friend or family member's) gender identity, ethnicity, race, religion or other characteristics.**You also have the 'right to know'.** This means that if police checks show that your current or ex-partner has a record of violent or abusive behaviour, and they believe you may be at risk, they may decide to proactively share that information with you. If you're worried that your current or former partner has been abusive or violent in the past, Clare's Law was created to formally give you the right to find out.

Prologue

ADEN

I check my gun once again, tucking it into the waistband of my dress pants and adjusting my stiff jacket to keep it hidden. A soft knock at the bathroom door makes me roll my eyes as I twist the faucet on, flicking my fingers under the water as I whistle to myself. I comb my damp fingers through my hair, tucking the blonde strands back into place. Another knock sounds, this time with more urgency, and I yank the door open with a smile.

"My apologies," I say, nodding my head to the scowling face of an older man. He rolls his eyes, brushing past me before I can step out of his way. Taking in my surroundings, I casually stroll through the extravagant home amongst the crowd of people. These rich families have everything, including an obnoxious fountain in the middle of their foyer. But I'm not here to complain about their expensive taste.

"Makes you wonder what somebody is hiding when they flaunt their wealth so carelessly." A soft voice says, catching me off guard in the chatter of conversation around me. A woman steps around me, smiling at me from the corner of her eye. She is wearing a pale pink gown that is strapless, showing off her gorgeous bronze skin. I watch her graceful movements as she sits on the edge of the fountain, stretching her legs out as she rolls her ankle, frowning at the heels she wears.

"Makes me wonder what type of woman willingly puts herself through so much pain for a pair of shoes hidden under your dress." I say, stepping closer. She giggles, and the sound is enchanting. I'm drawn closer to her, from the beautiful smile to the shy way she peers at me through her lashes.

"You've got a point about that."

"Aden," I say, holding my hand out. She places her hand in mine, and I brush a kiss across her knuckles, not missing the blush that stains her cheeks.

"Nina."

"A beautiful name for a beautiful woman." I say, shamelessly flirting. She grins, opening her mouth to speak, but snaps her jaw shut when she looks over my shoulder.

"Apologies, am I interrupting?" A man says, bumping his shoulder into mine as he steps past. Nina quickly stands, smoothing her dress as she nervously laughs.

"No David, I was just resting for a moment and this gentleman was making sure I was alright." She says in a placating tone. David grabs her upper arm roughly, jerking her to his side as he gives me a disgusted look.

"You can't stop lazing about, even for our engagement party?" He snaps while he drags her away. My hands flex as I reach for my gun, but Nina locks eyes with me over her shoulder. She smiles sadly as they leave, hurrying to keep up with his long strides.

"For a bunch of rich folks, the food sucks." Markus complains, walking past me with his cheeks stuffed. I'm still staring after Nina's retreating head of brown curls in the crowd when Markus pops his head in front of my face.

"Did you find the target yet?" He asks, green eyes shining in amusement. I roll my eyes, shoving past him. If I had known years ago that becoming best friends with Isabelle would mean working alongside her two husbands, I might have reconsidered our friendship. Or taking her on as my first serious job.

"David Killinger is just up ahead, but we can't exactly take him out with all these people watching." I mutter, staying far enough back that his bodyguards won't notice me, but close enough to keep an eye on them.

"Oh, so you were eye fucking his fiancé?" Markus says, smirking when an older woman gives him a shocked expression. Markus winks at her, taking the glass of champagne she was holding as we pass.

"Could you try to blend in a little better?" I clench my jaw, fighting the urge to shout at him. Markus sighs, dropping the glass to let it shatter on the floor. All eyes nearby turn to us, and I drag a hand over my face in irritation.

"You're so boring. Looks like your damsel might be in distress." He leans close, nodding ahead.

David has his mouth against Nina's ear, and to those around us in the formal ballroom, they appear to be two lovers sharing a secret.

But I know fear when I see it, even though Nina is putting on a brave face. The redness creeping up her neck and widened eyes tells the truth. Before I can follow them up onto the grand staircase, Markus grabs the collar of my jacket and pulled me to a stop.

"Now who isn't blending in?" He taunts. David lets go of Nina, the two of them facing the crowd. Somebody taps a glass, getting everyone's attention as David flashes a fake smile.

"Thank you all for joining us to celebrate the upcoming marriage between Nina and I. I am truly blessed to have a woman like her standing at my side." He beams at Nina, who smiles up at him, her arm linked through his. David waves his hand and the lights dim as the band strikes up a slow song. Markus nods to me and we split up, keeping our eyes locked on the couple.

David pulls away from Nina, leaving her standing on the floor as he makes his way to the open bar.

"Do you need a dance partner?" I ask, stepping up close to her. Nina smiles, but I can see the unshed tears in her eyes as she turns and walks away. That's when I notice that she's unguarded. This prick has left his bride to be completely vulnerable and it pisses me off. I easily follow her through the double doors, and out into the garden. She leans on the rail that separates the patio from the flowers that surround the garden. I keep my steps silent as I prowl behind her, giving her space while watching over her.

"If you're here to kill me, just get it over with." Nina says, her voice breaking as she turns to face me. The sight of tears tracking down her cheeks, dripping from her full lips, drags me closer. Further away from my mission.

"I would never hurt you, Nina." My words are so soft, I'm not sure she's heard me. She laughs, the sound humorless as she folds her arms over her chest.

"You're not on the guest list, are you? You're not with the caterers, and David is waist deep in debt to multiple mafia families. I am not stupid." She says, venom in her words. I shake my head, leaning against the rail next to her.

"No, I imagine that you're as smart as you are beautiful. David is tangled in more than just debt." I say, tucking a strand on her behind her ear. "Run, Nina. Find somewhere safe and get away from him." I say, turning to leave.

"Are you going to kill him?" She asks, catching my sleeve. I pull away, not looking back at her as I watch David step outside, his arm around Markus' shoulder as they laugh together. Markus winks at me while they step towards the gardens, overlooking the maze. David's bodyguards keep sharing worried glances, clearly on edge by Markus acting too friendly.

"There she is now, my lovely bride." David says, snorting a laugh as he waves a hand in her direction. Nina nods, a polite smile on her face as she nervously watches the interaction. That's when I notice that we are alone out here.

"Markus." I say. His smile drops from his face as he steps away from David, yawning as he stretches his arms above his head.

"I'm afraid my engagement gift isn't very exciting." Markus says. One of the bodyguards pulls his gun out, and I point the barrel of mine to his head and pull the trigger. The next few moments feel as if time has slowed down, and I watch Markus point his gun at David. But he's quick, slapping the weapon down and away from his chest.

The shot rings out, and David roars as he collapses face down and doesn't move. Nina slams into me, knocking the two of us to the ground as a third shot pops off, then a fourth. Warm blood drips down the sleeve of my jacket and Nina cries, clutching her shoulder as she rolls onto her back.

"Nina, look at me. You're going to be okay, just take slow and deep breaths." I try to reassure her, but I can see the terror and agony on her face. I take off my jacket, blanketing her with it as I rip the sleeve off of my button up shirt.

"Hurry up, Aden. We don't have much time." Markus helps me tighten the bandage around her arm as she continues to bleed, her skin taking an ashen tone. My heart pounds wildly in my chest as I scoop her up, stepping over the three bodies as I race after Markus. People have started coming out to check on the ruckus and we have to get her somewhere safe.

"We can drop her off at the closest emergency room," Markus starts to say.

"No, they'll think she had something to do with David's death, Nina will be in danger. She's coming with us." I cut him off, diving into the backseat of his car.

"You gave me shit for taking care of Isabelle against her will, now look at you." He smirks at me through the mirror.

"You kidnapped her!" I shout.

"Potatoes, tomatoes." He waves me off, nearly tipping the car up onto two wheels as he careens through traffic on the busy road. I cradle Nina's limp body in my arms, making sure not to jostle her too much as her closed eyes flutter.

"That's not at all how that saying goes, just get us back safely." I snap.

CHAPTER ONE

Aden

Watching her sleep next to me was the greatest feeling on this earth. Aside from our son's cries from the baby monitor. I jump up, rushing to scoop him from his crib in the nursery. Leo quiets down quickly, scrunching his face as he yawns. His soft curls make me smile as I brush my hand over them, cradling him to my chest as I rock softly.

"What do you say we let mommy get a little more sleep, buddy?" I ask, smiling down at him as he grunts and wiggles in my arms. I carefully lay him on the changing table, putting a clean diaper on him while he voices his displeasure with tiny whines and grumbles.

"You've got your mommy's hair, lucky boy. I hope you look exactly like her. She's the most beautiful woman I've ever seen." My voice is soft as I whisper to him, brushing kisses over his tiny head as I pick him up and sway in place.

"You boys having fun?" Nina yawns as she walks up, laying her head on my shoulder as she rubs her knuckle over his cheek.

"Now that our favorite person is here, hell yeah we are." I grin at her, placing a soft kiss to her lips. Leo whimpers, his lips curling into a pout as he works himself to tears.

"He wants something that I don't have the equipment for," I say, following her to the rocking chair as she takes Leo and starts nursing him. My phone dings, the screen showing Luna's name. I clench my jaw, fighting the urge to roll my eyes at my sister's name. The text message is short, and almost makes me smile.

"Jared finally came to his senses?" Nina asks, a knowing smile on her face.

"Apparently they're married, Luna didn't want a wedding and we are forbidden from interrupting their honeymoon for the next month." I shake my head, internally cringing. Nina smiles up at me, taking my hand in hers.

"I hope they have at least half the love that we share."

I kiss the back of her hand, turning the lights down as I leave them to snuggle and enjoy their quiet little bubble. I have work to do, which consists of finding out who keeps screwing with our deliveries before my dad rips me a new one. Or worse, our boss Lucian. Just as I open my laptop, my phone rings and I answer without looking at the screen.

"Well that was quick," Isabelle's voice carries over the phone and I can hear the smile in her tone.

"I'm in a bit of a time crunch here, Isabelle. Unless you want Lucian dad to skin me alive," I grumble, fingers skittering across the keys as I check our security cameras.

"I don't understand why everyone is so scared of him, my dad is just a big teddy bear." I can hear her husband Alec cough in the background, covering up his laughter.

"Towards you and Amelia, yes." He says, his voice getting louder as he gets closer to the phone.

"Aden, I spoke to Lucian earlier today. Our delivery of weapons has been intercepted again, and those trackers you placed went unnoticed.

I'm sending you the information now. Want me to pull Jared in?" Alec asks, but he's interrupted by the sound of a soft smack.

"We are not interrupting their honeymoon. Luna would kill both of you. I am a little hurt that they didn't even have a real wedding though." Isabelle huffs, and Alec blows out a grumbled sigh.

"Amelia is in need of a queen to attend her tea party, my darling." Markus' voice crackles over the phone as I turn on the speaker and set it on the table so I can open the files Alec emails me.

"Tell Nina I need some itty bitty baby snuggles," Isabelle reminds me before I hear her footsteps recede.

"I'll bring a team of my guys, you bring some of yours, and we can have a fun little circle jerk." Markus says. I fight the urge to hang up the phone, not in the mood for his careless attitude.

"Is that a no? Come on Aden, let's sword fight. Hey, ouch!" Markus says, the sound of a small scuffle followed by Alec's annoyed voice.

"Can you try being serious for just one moment?"

"Nope," Markus laughs, "Send me the time and coordinates, I'll be there." Markus calls out, his voice fading as he leaves. Alec curses under his breath, "Do you want me to come keep him in line?" He offers.

"Don't tell him I said this, but he's not intolerable. If Isabelle can put up with being married to the both of you, I'll manage. And the three of you agreed that one of you stays with Isabelle and your daughter at all times." I remind him.

"If you'd like, we could keep Nina and Leo company. It'll help with Isabelle's baby fever. Now Amelia is even begging Markus and I for a sibling." Alec offers and I relax slightly, knowing they would be safer.

"Thank you," I say, before the line disconnects and I stare at the address on screen, where the GPS says our shipment is.

Something about the random stolen equipment feels off, as if it's a diversion but nothing is happening and no ransom notes have shown up on anyone's door step. Maybe I'm just paranoid. I grab a hand towel, tying Nina's apron around my waist as I step up to the sink loaded with dirty dishes. Nina gets upset each time I leave for hands-on missions, while we were both raised in mafia families, she lived similar to my sister Luna.

A mafia princess, meant to be seen and not heard, and absolutely not allowed to participate in any of the family business. Nina knew what was happening, but seeing the dark side wasn't something she was familiar with. My sister dove headfirst into it, immediately taking on dangerous jobs and fighting for her place on the front lines.

Nina on the other hand, was tech smart and did incredible behind the scene work for each of us. She was an incredibly valuable asset, and I fell more in love with her every day. Her soft hands dig into my shoulders as she massages the tense muscles while I peer over my shoulder. Leo is strapped to her chest in a baby carrier, his face resting on her chest as he drools.

"Leo, you are one lucky guy." I say, shaking my head. "I want those back, one day." I say, giving her a serious look. Nina blushes, shaking her head as she sways gently, keeping our son content.

"Your daddy isn't going to get lucky if he comes home with even a papercut." She warns me, kissing the top of his head.

"I will always come home, this is my paradise." I say, turning back to the current chore.

CHAPTER TWO

Nina

Laying Leo in his crib and creeping out of the room without waking him was a rare feat, and I'll admit to doing a tiny happy dance when I tiptoed down the hallway towards my bedroom. Aden watches me, a lopsided smile on his face as I crawl into the bed and pull the covers over my head. He tugs the blanket away, leaning over me and brushing the stray hair away from my face.

"The Barones' will be here soon." He says, kissing my forehead when I frown.

"You'll come home to us," I say confidently.

"Always, baby." He kisses my cheek, slowly moving down to kiss my neck. "I have to make it back to worship my incredible wife," He murmurs against my skin, gently biting the soft skin. I suck in a breath as he pulls my shirt over my head, leaning back to gaze down at my body. I fidget, crossing my arms over my stomach but Aden grips my wrists in his hand, prying them away.

"Don't hide from me," He whispers, crawling further down the bed until his lips brush over the scar that cradles my stomach.

"I'm still self conscious over that." I whisper, nodding my head towards the slowly fading scar across my lower abdomen.

"This? This is just another reason for me to fall to my knees at your feet, Nina. What you sacrificed, what happened to your body, I am still in awe. You have given me the greatest gift I could have asked for and I will spend the rest of our lives proving to you how grateful I am." Aden kisses along the entire scar as I press my head back into the pillow and blink up at the ceiling when my pulse picks up.

"Look at me," He commands and my eyes snap to him.

"You are amazing, my love. I would give my last breath to feel your lips against mine." Aden's tongue darts out, tracing the edge of my panties as I watch, holding my breath.

"My Nina," he pulls my panties down my legs, "My wife," His breath fans over my bare skin, making me shiver.

"My love," He presses his tongue over my clit, making my back arch as I suck a breath in. I hear the click of a button, followed by a soft buzzing sound.

"Aden?" I ask, raising up onto my elbows in time to see the gleam in his eye as he presses my vibrating rose over my clit. The feeling overwhelms me suddenly, making my toes curl as I fall backwards onto the bed with panted moans. Adding to the pressure, he slowly works two fingers inside of me.

My fingers clutch the sheet as my body trembles, pleasure building at a quick pace that makes my heart pound until my chest aches. Aden curls his fingers just right, and a cry rips from my lips as release ripples through my body.

"That's it, good girl." He purrs the words, making goosebumps spring across my skin. Aden steps back, slowly twirling his tongue along his fingers as he stares down at me, a hunger in his eyes that reignites my desires.

"You are mine tonight, my love." He says, helping me stand and pressing a kiss to my forehead. I can't stop the giddy smile that curls my lips as Aden gathers clothes, helping me dress as he covers my skin in kisses. "Do you promise?" I taunt and he leans his back with a groan.

"How did I get so lucky?" He says, taking my hand in his as he leads me from the bedroom as the doorbell chimes through the house. I walk faster, even as my legs wobble and I have to lean against my husband more than once. Isabelle has become such a huge part in my life, and she's one of the few who sees my value as a person over financial.

"Come in," I say cheerfully as I swing the door open. Amelia runs through the open door, her dark curls bouncing as she bounds through. Alec nods to me, shaking Aden's hand as Markus rushes past all of us and the men follow after the two year old.

Isabelle shuts the door behind her and wraps an arm around my shoulder as we lean our heads together.

"I've missed you." I admit.

"Me too," She says as we join our husbands on the couch. Isabelle sits between Markus and Alec. I'll admit their relationship was a shock when I first met them, but now it feels so natural and all I can see is the love the brothers share for her.

I have to bite my cheek when I realize what Markus is wearing. Aden pinches the bridge of his nose as he leans back on the couch, draping his arm around my shoulders.

"Markus, what the fuck are you wearing?" Aden asks.

"Bad words," Amelia giggles, holding her stuffed bunny by his ear as she dances around the room.

"Amelia got these for me, thank you very much." Markus grins as we all stare down at his giant green froggy rain boots. "It's pouring out there and I hate wet socks." He huffs. Aden drops a kiss to the top of my head, "I'll be home before you know it, love." He promises as Markus whispers something in Isabelle's ear that makes her blush as she smacks his chest. As the two leave, I raise a brow at Isabelle.

"Do I want to know?" I taunt.

"No," Alec sighs, pulling his phone out and excusing himself from us. Isabelle jumps up to flop onto the couch next to me, a knowing smile on her face.

"What?"

"You look like sex," My jaw falls open at her accusation as I quickly look over to make sure her daughter didn't hear her loud whisper.

"Good for you, girl. You need a little stress relief. Have they been taking it easy on you since you're back to working on all the tracking and stuff?" Her tone is serious and I appreciate the concern, but wave her off.

"Aden won't let me touch the computer for more than an hour without hovering and telling me to put my feet up, drink water and whatever else he can think of. All of my work comes through him and I'm sure he's telling his father and your husbands no to anything he worries will be too stressful." I frown and Isabelle rolls her eyes.

"Tell him to stop hovering."

"It's not a bad thing, he just worries." But part of me wants him to back off, let me prove to him that I can handle everything.

"We can't just stop protecting you because you think there is no threat. The moment we let our guard down, something bad can, and will, happen." Alec strolls back in with his hands in his pockets, glancing between Amelia and Isabelle with a look of worry. It's the same look Aden gives Leo and I when he thinks I'm not paying attention. They really can't help but to see everything as a threat, considering the way they were raised.

Alec drops a package on the table, "Aden said you missed one of your packages. Apparently Isabelle isn't the only one who shops online too much." He smirks. I roll my eyes as I take it to the kitchen to grab my scissors and cut open the paper bag. I peer inside and immediately roll the bag up and shove it under the sink. My heart starts to thunder and I grip the counter while forcing myself to suck in shaking breaths. A tiny whine comes from the baby monitor.

"Leo is fussing, dibs!" Isabelle yells, and I hear her feet thunder up the stairs. I force myself to calm the panic rising in my chest as I get drinks for everyone and walk back to the living room.

CHAPTER THREE

Aden

We check the GPS signal one last time, convincing ourselves we must be at the wrong place. The tracker continues to flash on the screen, marking the coffee shop we are parked in front of. Markus and I share a look of uncertainty as we give the signal to our team to stay where they were, in their vehicles. We tuck our guns into our waistbands before stepping up to the doors.

"Welcome," A cheery barista smiles behind the counter as I glance around the room. Markus doesn't hesitate, ordering the both of us a drink with a bright smile. The quiet pace is filled with various people, studying late, reading a book and just going about their day. Hairs on the back of my neck raise up as a bad feeling grips me.

Markus shoves a cup into my hands, but I notice he isn't looking at me. His head is tilted as he stares at a woman seated near the windows with a book in her hands.

"I need to tell Isabelle there's a book out there with her name on it, literally." Markus smirks, nodding to the title on the book's cover,

'Our Darling Isabelle'. I snort a laugh while we both try to look around without being too obvious.

"We need to get this over with. I miss my girls." He grumbles at me as he drops into a small leather chair. I sit across from him as I take out my phone and frown when I see the tracker is moving around the building. I show the screen to Markus and he looks outside, and I can tell the moment he sees our target.

"Stop drop and roll, people." He shouts, tackling the girl next to us to the ground. I dive next to them as the glass window shatters inward, raining around us. Bullets fly through the air as we hear our teams return fire, slowing the assault. Markus moves his arm from the girl's head, and her eyes widen in shock while he fixes her glasses.

"Sorry about that," He winks, perking his head up to look at the name on her coffee cup and grabs her book to hand back to her.

"Aly? What a lovely name. Looks like your book survived. Stay down until you don't hear anymore shots, okay?" Markus says, plucking glass from her dark hair. She nods, jaw slack and eyes wide as he beams a grin at her.

"Good girl." Markus turns to me, "Let's move." He says as I jump up to follow him out. Wasting no time, we leap through the blown out windows and pound our feet onto the pavement while pulling out our guns. The parking lot is littered with broken glass from dark tinted windows, splatters of blood, but no bodies. A white car peels out as one of ours chases after them, and I know we won't have a chance to catch them in our massive SUV. Once we ensure the threat is gone, I kneel next to a crumpled piece of plastic with wires sticking out of it.

"The tracker," I pick it up, staring at the only lead we had. Markus curses beside me, kicking a rock across the parking lot in his frog rain boots. Another time and I would laugh at the sight, but right now failure is dragging me down as I stare at where the vehicles have vanished.

Markus' phone rings, and he answers by saying his name as we climb into our car. A flash of rage contorts his face as he hangs up, slamming the palm of his hand onto the steering wheel.

"Our guys said they caught up to them, but they were dead by the time they got the doors open. Crazy bastards killed themselves." Markus shakes his head, his usually carefree expression now tense. I groan, rubbing a frustrated hand across my forehead. Markus checks his watch, sighing as the sound of police sirens closes in on us.

"Time to go?" He gives me a cheesy grin, maneuvering us into the flow of traffic as I fight the oncoming headache I always get when I'm around the Barone's.

When we finally get back home, we are greeted by the sounds of our children. *Screaming.* We both speed into the living room, finding a very distressed Alec holding both children and looking frantic.

"I was holding Leo while Nina was in the kitchen getting a snack for Amelia, but Isabelle had to run to the restroom. Amelia doesn't like sharing Papa." Alec grumbles, shifting a fussing Leo into my arms as I smirk at him. Amelia is clinging to him, her red cheeks covered in tears as she stares daggers at me.

"Mean old Papa," Markus feeds into her dramatics, holding his arms out for her to dive into them.

"You're spoiling her." Alec grumbles, fishing in Isabelle's purse until he holds up a sucker. Amelia giggles and shoves away from Markus, who rolls his eyes.

"Yeah, I'm definitely the problem." He mutters. I hear a giggle and Isabelle runs to Markus, throwing her arms around his neck. Nina is much more reserved with guests here, but I step right up to her and hold her tight in my free arm.

"Did you miss me?" I ask, grinning as she blushes and nods when I press a soft kiss to her forehead.

"Amelia, you're going to have to get used to sharing Papa and Dada. Being a big sister means you'll have more responsibilities." Isabelle says casually. I can see the moment everyone registers the news. Nina must have known, since she was watching the brothers with amusement.

Markus turns towards Alec, both of them pointing fingers at each other simultaneously.

"This is your fault." They both shout, making Nina hide her face in my shoulder as she laughs. Isabelle was grinning, patting her stomach.

"Congratulations?" I say, raising a brow. Markus and Alec both broke, crushing Isabelle between them in a hug, Markus lifting her off her feet as Alec threw Amelia into the air.

"You're going to be a big sister, princess." Alec coos, the only time we see the softer side of him is with his daughter. I can see the excitement on everyone's face, instantly lifting the sour mood I had come home in.

As we say our goodnights and the Barone family head home to celebrate in ways I didn't need to know, Nina had become more quiet than usual. She took our baby to his room, and I found her still standing over his crib nearly an hour later. She startles when I brush her hair away from her neck and I take her hand in mine, gently pulling her to our room.

"Are you going to tell me what's bothering you, or do I have to lock you in here with me until you give in?" I taunt, lightly gripping her throat as I brush my nose over her cheek. Nina trembles in my grasp, but it wasn't from excitement. I quickly let go when she threw herself against my chest, burying her face against my neck as gentle sobs wracked her body.

"I've got you, sweetheart." I say, picking her up and carrying her to our bed. I rip the covers out of the way, climbing in while still holding her tight. When I toss the blanket over our heads, she pulls away to give a choked laugh and I feel her swiping at her cheeks.

"I'm sorry. I don't know what came over me." She murmurs. Nina was lying to me, but I wouldn't prod her. Not right now, at least.

"No, don't apologize for your feelings." I just hold her close, burying my face in her hair as sleep slowly pulls us both under.

Chapter Four

Nina

When Aden is snoring, I finally creep out from under his arm and blow out a breath as I close the bathroom door behind me. I pull out the burner phone that had shown up in the mail today, and with shaking hands, I power it on. The screen flashes, one un-opened message was waiting for me. Hesitation is beat out by curiosity as I click it. A picture of my sister, smiling bright as a man I had never seen before leans close, petting the big dog she was walking.

Her dog had pulled away from the man, his eyes wide and that told me more than anything how much danger she was in. Olivia was a soft girl, her skin a few shades darker than mine and eyes so dark I almost couldn't see her pupils. She was beautiful and kind, which is why I did everything I could to protect her.

I found one phone number saved. The crushing weight that I had run from all these years had finally caught up to me, and if I don't face this head on then my sister will suffer for my own mistakes. Leo's fussing came through the baby monitor, and I quickly shoved the cellphone under the sink, inside of my makeup bag. Aden jumps up, and I hear his sluggish foot fall as he drags himself to our son's nursery.

I caught sight of myself in the mirror and tentatively touched my wet cheek, not even realizing I was crying again.

"Nina, are you alright honey?" Aden calls, our son's cries coming closer to the bathroom door. I splash some cold water on my face, quickly patting it dry with the puffy gray towel and hanging it back up as I compose myself. When I step back into the bedroom, Aden is bouncing in place, rocking our still unhappy baby. He turns to me, a look of relief on his face.

"I didn't mean to rush you, baby. He's hungry, but I changed him and did my best." He says, waiting for me to get settled into bed before laying Leo in my arms. I beam a smile at him as I latch the baby on.

"You're amazing, Aden. I love you." The words slip through my tight throat and he sits next to me, pulling my back towards him to rub my shoulders.

"Something is bothering you, my love. What is it?" His words are gentle but I still flinch.

"I'm just exhausted," The words come easily, because they're not a lie. I am exhausted, but also terrified for my sister. For the beautiful family I've built here. Panic is trying to drag me under, but Aden's strong hands are slowly working my tension away.

Leo drifts back to sleep after he finishes eating, and I carefully carry him back to his crib. I know what I have to do, but that knowledge is weighing heavier with every breath. If Aden knew what was happening, he would wage a war to keep me safe but how many would die in the process? How many of my friends, family and people I've come to care for these past few years would I lose?

This was a sacrifice only I was willing to make and that knowledge steels my resolve. Aden is still watching me with cautious eyes, ones that are trained after years to perceive the slightest change.

To notice the twitch of a hand as an enemy reaches for their gun. To catch someone in a lie.

"We swore to never keep secrets." Aden says, his jaw clenched as I laid with my back against his chest, trying to keep a calm demeanor. I giggle, shaking my head as I pulled his arm around me.

"Aden, we're both exhausted. Leo's sleep regression hasn't been easy. But everything will be okay," *For the two of you, even after I'm gone.* A few moments pass until he blows out a frustrated breath, burying his face into my neck.

"You'll tell me eventually?" The question makes my heart melt as he tries to give me space.

"I love you," The proclamation is met with silence, and a night full of little to no sleep.

My coffee is far more bitter than usual, and it had to be from the barely concealed irritation Aden was carrying around. I was doing my best to move on as if everything is normal, and here he was throwing a wrench in those plans.

"Maybe I should cancel my appointment." Aden huffs, but I roll my eyes and wave a hand.

"You've been going on about this tattoo since Leo was born. Just go and enjoy being stabbed," I smirk, trying to ease the tension but it doesn't work. He glances at his phone again, and I sigh.

"I don't need a sitter. Leo and I are going to enjoy our day in pajamas lounging around the house." I try to calm his nerves. Aden gives me a long stare as he contemplates my words. He gives in with a sigh, stopping by the baby swing to kiss Leo on top of his head and stand next to me.

"I'll be checking in on you." He warns me, and I smile up at him, leaning close to kiss him before he walks out the door. As soon as his car pulls out of the drive, I sprint upstairs to grab the cell phone. When I pick it up, Leo starts crying and it feels as if he is trying to warn me.

But I power it on, and stare at the message now flashing on the screen. *Motherhood looks so good on you.* The attached image was through the window, taken just this morning of me holding my son. My skin crawls as I race back to see Leo with his lip curled and tears trailing down his cheeks. I scoop him up, rubbing my nose over his blonde curls as I rush to check the cameras. As I open my laptop, our surveillance video pops up across the screen. Nothing is out of the ordinary and I finally blow out a breath of relief.

I pull out the phone again, typing a message to ask them what they wanted.

But I don't get a response, as the day drags on and my anxiety spikes, nothing comes through.

The front door swings open, and I jump from the couch as fear ripples through my body. Aden is grinning as he closes the door, kicking it shut before taking long strides towards me.

"I missed you every moment I was gone," He mutters, pulling me into his arms as I try to hide my trembling hands. But Aden notices, as he does any subtle change. Holding me at arm's length, Aden's eyes scour my face as I try to put on a placating smile.

"You're afraid, Nina." His jaw clenches as he sees through my terrible acting. I wave a hand in the air, trying to pull away as his grip tightens on my shoulders.

"I was just worried because you were gone for so long," it isn't a complete lie, but Aden just frowns as I turn away, heading back to the living room where Leo is in his bassinet. I drop onto our couch, looking up at him expectantly.

"Are you going to show me?" I raise a brow and gesture to him. Aden sighs, shaking his head at my obvious change of subject. But he reaches a hand behind his head, pulling his shirt off in one smooth move and tossing it to the floor at his feet. My fingertips slip across my lips as I struggle to swallow, my throat feeling tight as I stare at his abdomen.

I stand, taking a step closer to him as my hands flatten over my lower stomach. I can feel Aden watching me, uncertain of my reaction. Tears slip from the corners of my eyes as I reach out and gently touch the fresh tattoo. Aden hisses in a short breath, but he doesn't pull away as I look up at his face.

"You got my name tattooed on you, in the exact shape of my scar?" I ask, my voice breaking. He nods, his warm hands cup my jaw as he pulls me closer until our chests touch.

"I could tell you a thousand times over how beautiful your scar is to me, but now I can show you." He says, his lips pressing in a lingering kiss on my forehead. Aden holds me tight, my face buried in his chest as I cry and for a moment my problems all fade away. They come crashing back when Aden pulls away, looking down at a security alert on his phone. His demeanor changes, and he's no longer my gentle husband. He's a ruthless member of the mafia, ready to protect his family.

"Nina, take Leo and go to the safe room. Take this," He presses a gun to my palm, ushering us towards our room.

"Aden, what is happening?" I ask, my voice steady even as my hands shake. He shows me his screen, and I watch as the cameras tick off, one at a time. Aden is dragging me to the stairs, with Leo cradled in his free hand and I can't tear my eyes away. The very last camera shows the guards booth at the end of our driveway, and there's a man lying limp on the ground with a dark puddle around him. Fear threatens to steal the air from my lungs as I run for our closet, watching Aden punch the numbers into a keypad that is set into the wall next to a hidden panel, just inside our walk-in closet. The internal latch pops with a soft click, swinging out just enough for me to grab it and pull it open. The dim lights flick on as I step inside, and Aden presses his lips to mine, then kisses Leo on the top of his head before sealing us inside.

"Aden, what are you doing?" I slam my hand to the door, barely able to hear his footsteps as they retreat. Tears blur my vision as Leo begins crying in my arms and I gently bounce him while turning to face the room. It's minimal, gray walls with one large bed on the far side. An average desk is set in with a large television mounted above a set of controls. I lay Leo into the small pop up crib, grateful that Aden added this in when we brought our son home.

Those days felt like a lifetime had passed since then. I sit at the desk and my fingers flow across the keys as I fight to regain control of our security system. After pounding out miles of code and getting to the point I nearly give up, the camera flashes back online. A ripple of movement catches my eye immediately and my relief is short-lived.

Aden has his gun raised, shouting something as he approaches a man on our front lawn. Something about him is familiar, but the camera quality isn't good enough for me to make out facial features. A row of our men stand behind Aden, their guns raised as they keep surveying the property, and that's when I catch sight of the dozens more crawling through the home, checking every potential entry point or hiding spot.

My pocket vibrates, nearly making me shoot from my chair and I stifle my scream with a hand slapped across my mouth. I pulled the phone out, hand shaking as I open the message. Tears continue to break free as I watch Aden pull the trigger, and the man's body falls to the ground.

This was all my fault, and if I didn't do something, the family I left and the one I created would be in danger.

Forgive me, Aden.

Chapter Five

Aden

I don't want to drag my ass out of bed, until I realize that I'm alone. After we cleared the entire property, I called in extra guards to be safe, Nina and I had fallen asleep in our bed. It wasn't easy for either of us to close our eyes. Every scuff and bump had us shooting from the bed, and I didn't think I would ever get any rest. But as I peeled my eyes open, the sound of Leo's cries dragging me from my bed, my heart knew that something was wrong.

I hum to him, bouncing my fussing baby as I search for his mother. My tired pace quickly turns into a jog as I call her name, waiting for her to pop up and break the tension that clouds my heart. But I knew she wasn't here, deep down. The house feels too empty and cold. My panic grows, gripping me with every step, each empty room mocking me as I sought the one person in this world who can give me peace. Nina is gone, and as I shout orders to anyone and everyone who was within ear shot, things continue to get worse.

One of my security personnel drops a phone into my outstretched palm. But it wasn't one I have seen before and I continue to stare at the crushed screen in my palm as I wait impatiently for my phone to charge enough to power it on. I dropped it in the chaos and forgot it last night, but now I was desperately hoping there was a reasonable explanation from Nina that I had missed.

My phone chimes, the screen flashing to life on the counter as I lunge for it. There's a message that I had missed, but it isn't from a number I recognize. Something tells me it's from a burner phone, one that I can easily trace but it will end up being useless. The screen makes my stomach twist and constrict, my mind refusing to accept it no matter how many times I read the words.

"You son of a bitch," I curse under my breath, barely resisting the urge to throw the device across the room. Nina is missing, and I am normally the one to take charge and lead at times like this. But here I am, knuckles white from how tightly I grip the countertop as I lean against it.

"Boss?" An unsure voice comes from the doorway, as I look up and nod my head to Clint. He steps forward, and shakes his head once, only confirming what I knew to be true. They hadn't found anything.

"Call Alec, we need help." I mutter, staggering to the couch as I drop into it. My body has become cold, as if all feeling had drained with my energy. I hear Clint talking into his phone, but my pounding heartbeat muffles everything else until a cell phone is shoved into my hand, and he walks away before I can argue.

"Aden, answer me or I will be on your doorstep. Clint said it's an emergency. Aden?" Isabelle snapped at me, her voice rising in concern.

"Nina is gone," my voice sounds robotic, even to me. Isabelle blows out a huff, not understanding the short response I gave her.

"I'm sure she will be back, did you guys have a fight? Where did she go, maybe she just needs somebody to vent to. You men don't make it easy, ya know." She rattles on, and I can hear her husbands arguing in the background.

"Somebody shut down our security last night. They killed one of my men, and now she's gone." I feel my throat tighten, but I bite back the agony when it threatens to pull me into the darkness.

Isabelle shouts something, muffling the phone until I hear the sound of a car door closing.

"Alec, I won't stay behind no matter how many times you threaten to tie me up. You're not scaring me, you're just making me horny so knock it off." She grumbles, and I roll my eyes at their neverending antics.

"What are you doing?" I ask.

"Be there in ten, maybe less. Markus is driving." The line goes dead as she hangs up on me. Clint takes his phone, dropping onto the chair across from me and pins me with a concerned look that only irritates me.

"I'm not going to fall apart, so stop looking at me like that."

"I sent word to your father. Vincent said he will gather a team to begin searching for her, but we need somewhere to start looking. Do you have anybody in mind that would want to hurt Nina or you?" He asks. I shake my head slowly, already having gone over every possibility.

"I haven't taken any jobs recently that warranted this. Nina doesn't have enemies." I say, struggling to think far back as I stare at the picture hanging on the wall. Nina smile's brightly back at me, with the image of our son in her arms and I stand proudly behind the two of them. I jump up and begin pacing the floor, spinning my wedding band with every step. My front door suddenly bangs off the wall, and Isabelle rushes to throw her arms around me.

"Don't worry, we're here." She tries to comfort me as I pat her back. Markus walks up, holding his fist up to bump against mine. Alec is staring at his screen, typing rapidly as he hangs back.

"Whoever hacked into your systems, wasn't fucking around. They knew how to cover their tracks and the one person who could help us is missing." Alec grumbles, finally looking up to catch my eye. "I remember waking up on the lawn to find Isabelle missing.We will find her." He says, nodding to me. I return the gesture, just as the baby monitor on the table lights up with Leo's cries

"I've got him, Amelia stayed with my dad." Isabelle says, walking away.

"We tried to call Jared, but they're still on their weird honeymoon thing." Markus chuckles, dropping onto the couch as he stares Clint down.

"What are you doing? Gather a team and start broadening your search. Canvass every fucking street, find security cameras or anything that could help. Go on," Markus dismisses Clint with a flick of his hand, and I roll my eyes at his abrasive cocky nature. Clint sighs, walking away to do exactly as Markus told him.

"He's one of my men and deserves more respect than that," I admonish him.

"Somebody on the inside helped orchestrate this." Alec says as he holds his cell phone out to me. A split second before the camera's cut out, a hooded man that was talking with the guard at our entrance gate pulled a gun and shot him. The guard was casual, leaning back with his arms crossed as if talking with a friend.

I curse under my breath, dropping my head into my hands as I try to recall anyone or anything out of the ordinary.

"The man I killed last night, we had never seen him before. He said I was going to pay for trying to kill their true leader. I thought he was just one of Stefan's lingering lackeys." I say.

"Luna and Jared killed Stefan. We watched the cleanup team take his dead body away to dispose of it, so what did he mean by 'trying to kill' this leader?" Markus grumbles, leaning back as he stares at the ceiling in thought. I notice the rainbow macaroni necklace he begins toying with around his neck and he smirks at me.

"Don't be jealous of my exquisite jewelry, one day your kid will make one for you. Not nearly as good as this one, but probably close."

He shrugs. I regret asking for their help with every passing moment. Isabelle rejoins us, humming as she rocks Leo.

"This little one is hungry, but Nina was nursing." she frowns, brushing a thumb over his round cheeks. Guilt pulls me to my feet as I realize that I didn't consider what I was going to feed my own son until his mother came back. Because she was coming back.

"Aden, I brought a can of formula. You've got enough on your plate and I figured it would be better safe than sorry." She tries to reassure me as she grabs her purse, carrying the canister to the kitchen as she readies him a bottle. Wherever Nina is, I am going to hunt her down and bring her home. Any who raise a hand to her, or stand in my way, will be nothing more than another dead body for me to step over.

Chapter Six

Nina

The car ride is long, and I have to pee, but I won't dare speak with this man's hand gripping my knee. His hand was scarred, the fingers crooked from years of fighting and who knows what else he had been doing since I saw him last. My jaw is throbbing, but my hands are tied securely together and I'm afraid to move, let alone touch the swollen lump. As we slow down, reaching a private jet, I feel my stomach drop. My sister is standing, her spine straight with a polite smile as the man next to her holds his gun to her temple.

"Olivia," her name is nothing more than a breath on my lips, but the man next to me lets out a boisterous laugh as if my suffering is enjoyable. For him, I'm sure it is.

"Isn't she beautiful? We both know I like women with dark hair and little more curves than that. But I told you that you had more motivation to behave than you expected. Come on now, we have a wedding to plan." His hot breath fans my neck as he leans close and I can't help but to clench my eyes shut as he drags his tongue over my neck. I jerk away and know I've made a mistake.

"Your manners have devolved from the company you have chosen to keep." He spits the words and grips my hair. Blinding pain erupts across the left side of my face as he slams my head against the window. I curl into a ball, crying out from the pain while trying to shield myself from more blows.

"Listen, baby, I don't like hurting you. What I do is for your benefit, to remind you of who you are." He almost sounds remorseful, but I had spent enough time with David Killinger to know better. He didn't feel remorse for being a monster. When the car stops, David drags me through his door and pulls me towards the plane while I struggle to match his massive strides. As we board the plane he shoves me into a seat and buckles me in. I swallow down the bile that rushes up when he tries to brush his lips against mine, trying to pry my mind away. David sighs, dropping into a chair next to me as he pulls out his phone.

I watch in horror as my sister is dragged onto the plane and shoved into the seat on David's other side.

"Little family reunion, how sweet. Little Olivia here has been missing you, nearly as much as I have. Of course, she's just not the same as you." He purrs, reaching towards my sister's face.

"No," I say without thinking, lunging towards them. Olivia's eyes widen a fraction as she shakes her head at me but it's too late. David's lips split into a malicious grin as the plane begins to take off, ripping me away from my family. I'm caught in his trap and he knows I won't do anything to endanger my sister.

My original plan was to play along, kill him in his sleep and escape back to my life. All of these years that I have spent safe and protected in Aden's arms has made me forget how smart David is. But he was meant to be dead after Markus shot him. Aden followed up to ensure it. As if he could tell what I am thinking, David reaches up and starts popping open the buttons of his blue dress shirt.

I look away, earning more of his disturbed laughter as he stands to get right in front of me, gripping my chin to wrench my head back.

My eyes lock immediately to the mottled scar, just below his left collar bone. The gunshot that I find myself wishing would have killed him until tears well in my eyes.

"Seeing you so overcome with joy that I lived is so touching, baby. It almost makes up for the betrayal of you marrying another man and letting him fuck you when I own you." He leans close, until his breath fans over my face, "I'll make sure you forget him, you useless whore. You fucking belong to me." My sister sniffles, and I look away from David to see her struggling to hold back tears.

"Everything will be alright, Olivia." I try to comfort her, grateful that David releases his grip on me and takes his seat. She closes her eyes, taking a deep breath before she opens them again. Her prim and proper mask is back and my pride flares to life.

"When we land, the two of you will earn your fucking place in my home. One of you will keep my bed warm every night, so I suggest you do exactly as I say, Nina." David warns me before motioning for his personal flight attendant. She flutters over him, bending low to give him a generous show of cleavage as she leans across his lap to set a glass of liquor in his cup holder.

"This is what a good girl does," He murmurs, winking at the woman as she walks away, flashing me a pitying look. The pain in my chest only grows the longer we stay in the air, and the further Olivia and I are taken from home. But I had made this decision, and now is not the time for regrets. The flight drags on while also feeling too short, and I dig my nails into the seat as the plane bounces along the runway. David has his hired muscle escort us off the plane and shove us into another car, but this time Olivia and I are together as he climbs into the backseat.

I take her trembling hand in mine, squeezing tight to remind her that I will always protect her. She is going to leave here the moment I see an opening. I spend the car ride fantasizing about watching David choke on his stupid cigar, the noxious smell making Olivia and I cough every time he rolls his window up just to taunt us.

I'm almost grateful when we pull through a massive pair of gates at the end of a driveway. The house itself would be beautiful if I didn't know what awaits us once we are inside, with palm trees swaying in the gentle breeze next to the white two story building. I take a deep breath, noticing the smell of salt that the wind carries from the ocean nearby. My teeth clamp down onto my lip as I imagine throwing David to the sharks beneath the waves.

Aden and Leo would love it here. The thought strikes me, sudden and sharp enough to steal my breath away. David grips me by my elbow, dragging me towards the massive double doors on the font of the beachside house. The paved pathway that leads towards the front door splits off in two different directions, one towards the beach and the other behind the house.

My curiosity stays silent, because I knew David wasn't going to risk me getting away anytime soon. As we step inside, I notice he has more guards than ever before. Two standing outside the house, an additional two just inside the door and dozens more milling about the property. He knows I won't go far, not with the way one of his men is gripping my sister's arm in his massive hand. If it was painful, she did an incredible job of hiding it.

"Come now, my little butterfly. Don't stray too far or I'll have to break your wings." David says, flashing me another bright smile. When our engagement was first announced, I remember thinking he was handsome and I was actually grateful to be matched with a man so high within his family's ranks. That dream crashed the first time he threw me to the floor for laughing at his friend's joke. He swore it wouldn't happen again, and I knew better than to breathe a word of his actions to anyone.

At the top of the grand staircase, I'm faced with another massive sitting room with multiple branching doorways. The first few doors we pass are shut, and I don't ask what is hidden behind each of them. One door in particular stands out, instead of white it's a dark oak and I know what's behind this one. David swings it open, shoving me inside with a smirk.

It's his bedroom. And my new jail cell. The room would be beautiful in any other situation, with vaulted ceilings and a miniature chandelier that hangs above the massive four poster bed.

But the walls catch my attention more than anything else. They're covered with photos, news clippings and every bit of information about my family. I clutch the front of my shirt when I see pictures of me on my wedding day, with Aden's face torn away. My fingers claw at the fabric of my shirt as I struggle to breath when I see photos of my family, with innocent little Leo scribbled over, and Aden's face smeared with red ink X's. David drags me forward, towards the corner of the room that has a small chaise next to a long chain that ends in a cuff.

I allow him to shove me to the cushion, and hold my left ankle up without even being asked. I keep my face impassive, with a tight smile. *See? I am a good prisoner, so let Olivia go home.* David laughs as he wrenches me back up and waves to the tall man with bright blue hair to bring Olivia over. He puts the cuff on her, gently setting her foot down as he steals a quick glance up at her face.

David throws me onto the bed, making me bounce as I grip the blankets for support. The sound of a metal chain rattles, scuffing over the wood floors before I feel the cold press of it clasping to my ankle. Unlike his friend, David isn't gentle and slams it against my protruding bone, making me clench my teeth against the pain.

This was going to be Hell, but I would endure it. For my family. For my husband and son.

CHAPTER SEVEN

Aden

My hands are shaking as I stare down at my son, sleeping in his car seat. After two days with no leads, I have to get help from my sister and her husband. The front door swings open, a pissed off giant standing in the frame as he looks me over with irritation. Jared is well over six feet tall, with dark brown hair that has specks of gray that trails into his beard, and a muscular build that I can admit is intimidating most days. But I have come to regard him as a friend, until he kidnapped my sister after he caught her stalking him. I raise my gun, pointing it at Jared while he snorts a laugh and continues giving me a bored expression.

"Where the fuck is she?" I ask him, not seeing or hearing her in the house. I haven't slept in days, and my exhaustion was getting the best of me but I didn't have time to play this game.

"That thing isn't loaded." Jared mutters, easily slapping the gun from my hand and sending it clattering to the floor. I frantically hush him as I bounce Leo in his carseat to try and keep him sleeping.

"How did you know?"

"You bit my head off for holding Amelia with a gun in my holster when she was that size. You also wouldn't have brought the baby if you were expecting a fight." He rolls his eyes in irritation.

"You got me there, but something has come up that I couldn't talk about over a phone call. I didn't know what else to do." I frown, swaying Leo as he begins fussing.

"Come in and have a seat. I'll make sure Luna puts clothes on when she gets out of the shower."

"Am I interrupting?" I taunt.

"Yes," Jared snaps as he stomps up the stairs. I take a slight joy from irritating the big guy as I step into their living room. This home fits Luna so well, the walls different shades of dark green and the furniture all black with pops of white. Even the wood floors are dark. I lean back on the couch, my eyes becoming heavy as I lay Leo next to me. Going multiple days without sleep is catching up to me, but I couldn't rest without Nina.

I lean my head back on the couch, sinking into the plush fabric as I begin drifting off.

My eyes fly open as I reach outwards, panic gripping me when I realize I've fallen asleep with the baby. Except he's gone now, too.

"Leo?" I shout, jumping to my feet and tripping over his empty car seat. I race towards the kitchen, barging into the room with fear pulsing in my veins.

"You can't just fall asleep on the couch with a baby. Especially my couch." Jared snaps at me, handing him to me.

"I know that. Things have just been hard at home and nobody is really sleeping much." I tell him, still upset with myself for falling asleep. That's when I notice Luna, and she reaches out to squeeze my arm. She brushes her pale hair away from her face, looking at me with sympathy in her blue eyes that match my own, one appearing brighter with the darkened and ridged skin around it.

Her scars are still healing, fading more each time I see her. She doesn't hide behind her hair now, as she ties it proudly back and holds her head high. The burns along the side of her face haven't changed her for me, but I can see the way Jared stares at her in wonder. His expression is so full of adoration, it pains me to be in the same room as them. Luna motions for her nephew, beaming a bright smile up at me.

"Come to auntie, let daddy get a cup of coffee and we can talk." She coos, sniffing his head.

"Why do they do that?" Jared mutters, turning to pour me a cup of coffee. I shake my head, happily taking the mug he offers me.

"Apparently, it's that new baby smell." I shrug, still not understanding it much myself, even after Nina explained it to me.

"Won't be long before you guys have one of your own," I comment, raising a brow when Jared tenses and I step past him, into the living room. Leo takes that moment to let out a shrill cry, balling his tiny fists up as tears pool down his cheeks.

"Or not," Luna mutters, quickly shuffling the baby back to me. Jared pulls her into his lap in the large recliner as I take my seat on the couch, picking up the bottle Jared had set down for me. I catch Luna snatching Jared's cup of coffee from his hands, and a twinge of jealousy rears its head.

"You don't like creamer." Luna accuses him.

"No, but you do." He chuckles.

"You knew I was going to drink your coffee."

"I feel like I'm intruding." I grumble, rocking Leo as I shoot dirty looks at Jared.

"You are." He says, earning a smack from Luna for it.

"We've got a problem," I finally say, holding my phone out for them to take.

"Who sent this?" Jared asks, staring at my phone.

"Give back what was never yours in the first place or lose everything?"
Luna reads out loud, shaking her head at the message.

"I don't know, but Nina is missing. She disappeared two days ago,
right after I got this message. I need help." I admit, my voice breaking
as I lock eyes with Leo. He peers up at me with untainted innocence,
but even I know he misses his mother. Jared stands, clapping a hand
on my shoulder as he pulls his phone out.

"Let me call Alec and Markus. We'll help you find her and figure
out what's going on." He says, stepping from the room as he presses
his phone to his ear. I blow out a breath that I had been holding, afraid
that he would turn me away or accuse Nina of leaving. Luna stands,
pacing the floor as she bites her lip.

"Lunatic," Jared calls from the other room, peering in to point at
her in warning. She sticks her tongue out, but I notice she stopped
biting her lip.

"Are you happy?" I ask her, catching my sister off guard. She stalls,
looking at me then back to where Jared has disappeared.

"I've never been happier," She says with strength and confidence.

"I'm glad you two worked everything out. He's good for you." The
admission comes easy and Luna gives me a bright grin.

"Before we do anything, you need a shower and a nap. Let us take
care of Leo. You'll be useless if you fall over from exhaustion and you
get really bitchy when you're tired." She says. I shoot her an angry
glare, only proving her point when Jared rejoins us.

"She's right, Alec and Markus will be joining us later on. Take the
spare room, don't touch my fucking soap." He huffs, stopping to
murmur something in Luna's ear that makes her blush fiercely as she
takes Leo once again.

"Don't threaten to breed me while my brother is listening," she
hisses.

"I didn't hear a word he said, but thank you for lining my therapist's pockets. You're both sick," I stomp towards the stairs, ready to be away from the two of them.

CHAPTER EIGHT

Nina

F ive days of being trapped here, and I am already losing strength and resolve to escape. David stands in front of the bed where I am sitting with a twisted look of pride in his eyes as he throws the lacy scrap into my lap. I had tried to shower, with Olivia guarding the door, but David's guards had told him immediately.

"I told you, if you want a shower, you'll earn it. Those are the clothes you'll be wearing when you get out." He shrugs as if it's an easy decision. I neatly fold the clothes and lay them on the bed, trying not to anger him.

"I'll be fine," I say. David sighs, stepping close and snatching me by the throat as he rips me off the bed and throws my already sore body to the ground. My shoulder takes the brunt of the impact and I'm unable to stop the soft cry that escapes. I notice the same guard from earlier steps in front of Olivia, almost as if he's protecting her. The plans that I had been forming changed drastically when I realized that he was infatuated with my sister. We would use it to our advantage when the time came to get her out of here.

David isn't going to let her leave, I know better than to trust his lies even if we have been apart all these years. I try to keep my calm, not wanting to let him enjoy my suffering more than I have to. David wrenches me up by my elbow, throwing me towards the bathroom without any care. Olivia leaps forward and catches me before I fall a second time, and I hold her tight out of fear he might retaliate against her.

David kicks my chain, nodding to the guard that has a soft spot for Olivia.

"Percy, unlock her. She isn't going to shut the door, and I want you to keep watch." He demands, glancing over his shoulder to smile at me as he leaves the room. Percy blows out a breath, brushing his hand through his blue hair.

"You heard the boss. I'll turn my back to give you privacy, but don't make me regret it. The window is sealed shut." Percy warns me as he gently uncuffs my ankle and massages the tender skin.

"I wouldn't leave without my sister." I tip my head to Olivia before walking into the bathroom. True to his word, Percy stands with his back to me and starts a conversation with Olivia.

"David will send you home in no time, sunshine." he reaches forward, brushing away a strand of hair from her eyes. I quickly shed my clothes and pull the glass shower door shut, before David sends in a guard that isn't as considerate as this one. My breasts ache, the tightness within them becoming unbearable as I massage and try to squeeze all the excess milk out. My sweet little Leo, this is just another reminder. Every morning I wake up with my shirt soaked and stuck to me, and my breasts throbbing. I feel like that alone has been a deterrent for David to keep his hands off of me, but it wouldn't last.

Even with hot water bursting across my skin, I still feel frozen. Every single toiletry is the exact kind I have at home. David has been watching me for so long, and none of us ever noticed. The idea makes my empty stomach churn and I cover my mouth, slowly kneeling on the floor as I let my despair drag me under.

I don't give myself very long, finishing up and stepping out to grab the plush towel waiting for me. Percy awkwardly hands me a bundle of clothes, and I can't find my old ones anywhere. Olivia is curled up on her couch, snoring softly.

"Boss demanded the old clothes be destroyed. He said you'll be given proper attire, though." His voice isn't reassuring and he won't look me in the eye. The proper attire is a skin tight dress that will barely cover my ass, no show panties and no bra. I curse under my breath as I dress, my patience reaching its limit.

"Nina?" Olivia's sleepy voice pulls me back to the room as she yawns, stretching her arms above her head. I notice a second pile of clothes, breathing a sigh when I notice her dress is longer and she's been giving real undergarments.

"Boss left some fresh clothes for you, sunshine." Percy carries them into the bathroom, getting her towel out and starting the shower.

"He's so kind," Olivia mumbles, her eyes popping wide when she notices my clothes.

"Not a word about the dress, Liv. Big blue didn't do any of that for me, I think he has a soft spot for you." I eye him warily, not sure if his interest is a good thing. She shakes her head, picking at the skin around her nails as he steps out of the bathroom.

"Can't imagine anyone has any good in them if they're in the company of that monster." Her voice is soft, but I know Percy heard her when he huffs out a breath. I drop onto the bed, peering out the windows to watch the sky darken. My mind begins to drift, imagining what Aden and Leo are doing. Aden must have torn the house apart by now. I really hope Luna will be able to bring him back from the edge.

Tears burn at the back of my throat when I realize how badly I want him to come for me, while praying he stays away. I can't live in a world without Aden in it, and I would trade my freedom a thousand times to ensure he and our son had long lives.

The door swings open, and I quickly brush away my tears when David walks in. His gaze ripples across my exposed skin, leaving me feeling dirtier than I had before my shower.

"You're joining me for dinner, wife." He says, holding his hand out. I glance towards the bathroom, grateful that Percy blocks the entire doorway with his broad frame. David waves a hand, dragging me to the hallway.

"I'll have something sent up for her meal. Unless you'd prefer I bring her instead?" He offers. I stop struggling against his hold, the fight leaving me in one sudden breath. "Such an obedient little thing." David snorts a laugh as we round the bottom of the stairs, heading to a part of the house I have not yet seen. I don't get a grand tour, instead I'm dragged towards the back door that leads to the yard, my bare feet padding over the cold floor. As we step outside, my heart sinks a little at the sight of massive walls surrounding the entire property, topped with barbed wire.

"Even if you escape, you will never be able to get away from me." Davids leads me towards a small round table that is surrounded by candles.

"What is this?" My voice is more nervous than I intended.

"A romantic dinner with my soon to be wife, obviously." He pulls my chair out, waving a hand for me to sit. This all felt like a final meal before the end of my life.

CHAPTER NINE

Nina

This is a nightmare. I cradle my arm to my chest, blowing on the welted red skin. David lost his temper when I didn't eat fast enough, and he held his fork over the flames of a candle, slamming it to my wrist before I could react.

"You do this shit to yourself, Nina. I hate correcting you, but one day you will learn not to push my buttons." He breathes hard, his knuckles turning white from how hard he grips the table. The only sounds are the waves on the ocean and my soft whimpers. All I can smell is my burnt flesh as I hold my wound close, realizing that I might break sooner than later if this continues.

"Go get her the medical kit. I've lost my appetite." David sighs, crossing his arms as he stares past me. "I was thinking of adding some flowers. This yard feels so bleak, don't you agree?"

I choose my words carefully, ensuring my voice is steady when I speak. "Flowers are a nice idea," I say.

"I'll have some brought in. You and Olivia will plant them tomorrow. Maybe we could get a dog. Would a dog make you happy, baby?"

"Any gift you give me would make me happy," I grit my teeth, the lie tasting bitter as I bite my pride.

"There's my good girl. Prove to me that you can take care of this puppy and we'll start discussing babies. We will have three or four, of course." He chuckles, rising from his seat and dropping a kiss to my head. I stop myself from flinching away by digging my nails into my arm as he kneels next to me, taking the med kit from his guard when he returns.

"Oh I hope this doesn't leave a scar, baby. I don't think I could stand seeing your pretty skin ruined." He frowns, carefully tending to the injury that he inflicted. I keep my eyes cast down towards his feet. When he's done, David leaves without another glance in my direction as he answers his phone. I stare up at the dark sky, smiling at one small victory that he apparently doesn't know about.

Leo was an emergency c-section, and there were complications that ended with a hysterectomy. I wouldn't be having another child and that was fine for Aden and I. We only wanted our little boy anyway. Another guard comes up, offering me his arm. I take it, peering at him from the corner of my eye as he guides me inside. He's broad shouldered, his head shaved bald and a skull tattooed on the back of his head.

"My name is Grayson, ma'am. You can call me Gray." He says, his voice deep and gravely. He opens each door, slowing his pace to match mine as he guides me back to my room. Olivia is sitting on the couch, staring down at her clasped hands when we enter the room.

Percy steps forward, bumping his fist to Grayson's as he leaves the room.

"Percy said Grayson is kind and that we will be safe with him." Olivia says, smiling up at the mountain of a man. He sighs, shaking his head as he closes the door.

"Percy is soft. He shouldn't be here in the first place, he needs to stop running that jaw." He grumbles.

"Why does he work for somebody like David?" Olivia whispers as if she's afraid somebody will hear her. Grayson shifts uncomfortably, tilting his head as he listens for any sounds in the hallway.

"We aren't all beasts, ma'am. Some of us did what we had to for somebody we love." He looks at me, nodding in respect. I sit on the edge of the bed, searching for the metal cuff. That's when I notice Olivia isn't wearing one and they've been removed from the room.

"What happened to our chains?" I ask.

"David had them removed. He said that you weren't going any-where." Olivia says, not looking at me.

"Liv? What is it?"

"He said that Aden isn't looking for you. That he's given up al-ready." Her words are strained, but they still hit me as if she'd screamed them. I shake my head, standing to pace. For the first time in days, a giggle bubbles from my lips as I grip my elbows.

"Aden would never give up." I stop pacing, glancing at Grayson and decide not to say anything else.

He quirks a pierced brow while staring at me. "To David, it looks like Aden has given up. But a real man would scour every inch of the earth to find the woman he loves." He looks away standing straighter when we hear footsteps outside. Olivia and I quickly sit on the bed and I take her hand in mine. David steps into the room with a yawn, wearing black silk pajama bottoms as he tilts his head.

"I've never had two sisters at once."

"No," The word rushes from me before I can stop it. Olivia tenses, her eyes wide as she stares straight ahead while holding her breath. David barks a laugh, shaking his head as he drops onto the bed next to me.

"Of course my girl doesn't want to share me. Have it your way, baby. I wonder which one of the men wants a turn with her tonight." He leans around me to grin at my sister and her hand shakes in mine. My mind races as I try to think of any way to protect her from this, from those monsters that wait just beyond the door.

"She hasn't been married off yet, I bet the boys would tear eachother apart to get her as a wife." He reaches forward, but I take his hand in mine and turn to block her from his view.

"I'm not sure she is ready for that." I say, rubbing his hand between mine. Percy returns at that moment, bringing in multiple bags with labels from different clothing shops.

"Percy, take Olivia to your room. She's yours for the time being." David waves his hand. Percy no longer has the soft kindness in his expression as he grins, his eyes tracking Olivia with each step. My heart thunders in my chest, but Olivia stands and walks to him willingly without daring to lock eyes with me.

At the last moment, with Grayson following behind him, Percy catches my eyes, nodding once. My moment of relief is short lived as David's hand lands on my thigh, sliding towards my crotch. I stop his movement with my hand, blocking him from reaching any closer as I try to stand.

"I'm just really exhausted," I say. David stands up, wrapping his hand around my throat as he slams me backwards on the bed.

"I'm not going to be fucking patient forever, Nina. It's been too long since I've felt your legs wrapped around me." His grip on my throat isn't painful, just enough to keep me pinned in place as he forces his body between my knees to grind against me. I turn my face away, tears brimming my eyes as he presses his hard length against me. His free hand palms my breast over my clothing while his tongue brushes across the shell of my ear.

He stops, dropping his head to my shoulder with a sigh as I wait, my body shaking as the moments tick past.

"You'll beg me to fuck you, Nina. When you finally do, it'll be the sweetest reward I've ever earned." His voice is soft, kind as he kisses my cheek and climbs off. He pulls out a matching pair of silk pajamas, lifting my ankle to pull them up. He peppers both legs with gentle kisses, his hot breath fanning over my thighs as he tops, staring up at me with his mouth inches from my core.

With a crooked grin, he pulls the pants on and holds his hand out. I take it, allowing him to pull me to my feet as I wait for his kindness to end. He takes my dress in his hands and pulls it over my head. I quickly cross my arms to cover my chest, but his eyes are glued to the scar between my hips that was mostly covered by my pants.

"What happened to you?" He asks, pushing the top of my pants down to get a better look.

"It's from when I had my son," I stare up at the ceiling. He hums, nodding as if it makes perfect sense.

"I won't let that man ever touch you again. He tainted you inside and out." David spits the words as he pulls the shirt over my head and pulls the covers back.

"You'll sleep in my arms or you'll sleep on the floor," He tells me, rounding the bed as I crawl under the blankets. His arm snakes around my waist, pulling me to his chest as his fingers lazily brush across my hip.

"Sleep, my love." He says, rubbing his nose along my neck. In the dark, with the blankets covering us and the sound of our breathing, I can almost imagine it's Aden holding me. His warmth pressed to my back, protecting me. Keeping me safe.

CHAPTER TEN

Aden

Sweat drips into my eyes, but the pain radiating from my ribs is the only thing I can focus on. Each breath hurts and I'm sure I've broken at least a rib, but I won't let that stop me. I stand taller, swiping a hand across my brow as I throw aside my ripped shirt. Markus rolls his eyes, licking the blood from his split knuckles as he watches me.

"I'm not going to fight you naked, no matter how much you beg." Markus grins.

"Shut the hell up," I snap, launching myself towards him. He catches me, side stepping and using my momentum to twist and throw me to the floor.

"You're fighting with emotion, Aden. This is senseless and helps neither of you." Alec says, sitting in a lawn chair as he sips his whiskey with a bored expression.

"He told me to give up!" I roar, jumping from the grass to tackle Markus. He lands under me with a grunt, driving his elbow back to land on my tender side. The air rushes out between my teeth with a hiss as I roll away from him. The two of us are breathing hard, and Markus shakes his head as he stands and brushes his pants off.

"I told you to stop looking in obvious places, you shitstain. Whoever has her, has taken her somewhere secluded. Her useless father still hasn't found any trails on where Olivia is or who could have taken her. Considering he didn't want you two to be married in the first place, have you considered daddy dearest?" Markus holds his hand out, helping me stand.

He has a point, Nina's father has never liked me or my family. We aren't high ranking leaders, like Alec and Markus. But I shake my head and dismiss the thought, especially since Nina's sister Olivia is missing as well. Luna rushes out the back door with her laptop in her hands, interrupting us.

"I found something! Wait, were you two wrestling shirtless? You really miss Nina enough to start playing for the other team?" Luna quirks her brow, and Jared's laugh booms from behind her as he smirks at my expense.

"Fuck all of you, I'll find my wife on my own." I throw my hands up, but turn back to stare at my sister.

"You found something?" I ask, hope flaring to life as I rush to her side. Luna kneels next to a table, setting her laptop on it as her fingers fly across the keys.

"Look at this, I checked flight logs for the day that Nina disappeared. Even private aircrafts have to be registered and have a log of flight plans. There was one that caught Isabelle's eye. Read this one, and the name of the aircraft." She highlights a chunk of text as I lean closer.

Rage erupts from every inch of my body as I read the name, over and over. The lines blur as my arms shake from how tightly my hands are fisted.

"Shit," Markus mutters, and Alec is already on the phone.

"Killinger, yes he is fucking alive. I don't give a shit, find him. I'm sending you where he landed. Go," Alec shouts into his phone.

"David Killinger was her fiance, right?" Luna asks. I nod, dropping into a chair as I grip my head in my hands. He abused Nina before, he was a violent and disturbed man before Markus shot him. Now he had her, my beautiful and soft Nina. My paradise was being ripped apart every moment I was away from her, and she had been trapped with him for a week now.

"I shot that bastard, he should be dead." Markus is pacing, his hands fisting then relaxing again as he stomps across the grass.

"Daddy?" A tiny voice calls, halting each of us in our tracks as Amelia rushes towards Alec. Isabelle steps towards me, setting the baby monitor next to me as she puts her hands on my shoulders and forces me to look at her.

"Nina is a strong woman, Aden. Don't you dare sit here and think she's broken. Get the fuck up so we can bring her home." She tells me, and I see the redness in her eyes. Nina isn't just my family. She belongs to all of us. I nod, standing as I grab my discarded shirt from the ground.

"I'm dropping Leo off at my parents, and I'm bringing my wife home." I tell them as I rush through the house. She just needs to hang on a little longer, after she comes home, I am never letting anyone get between us again.

My father tried to stop me, more than once. But my mother grabs me in a swift hug before taking Leo away. "Come home to us, and bring this little guy's mommy back." She calls over her shoulder to me. My father lifts his cane, pressing it to my chest as he stands straighter to look me in the eyes.

"That monster won't drop his guard a second time, boy. He will be expecting you if you rush in without using that head of yours." He warns me.

"Vincent. Give the kid a break. He's smart and brave, he helped rescue my little girl once upon a time." Isabelle's dad, Lucian, says as he joins us in the entryway brushing a hand over his black suit. His dark hair is slicked back, and his black beard is clipped short to frame his large jaw. Lucian commands respect, from his personality down to the way he towers over everyone with broad shoulders that can carry the weight of the world on them. The intimidating man looks me over, frowning at my busted lip and overall disheveled appearance. I bow my head in respect to him.

"Did you scrap with Markus or Jared?" Lucian grins at me.

"Markus," I sigh, crossing my arms as he laughs.

"If it was Luna's husband, he wouldn't be conscious yet." Vincent smirks, waving me off as he runs a hand through his gray hair and leans on his cane.

"Be on your way, but be safe." My father tells me, but Lucian holds his hand up to stop me from leaving. I grind my teeth in irritation at being held up but I don't dare turn my back on a mafia leader.

"Bring the both of them home, alive. Kill everyone else there. No loose ties." Lucian gives me a serious look, his black hair falling into his eyes as he waits. I bow to him, "Yes sir."

By the time I reach my car, Alec is already leaning against it with his tilted as he stares over my shoulder.

"Mr. Kane," He says with an air of boredom. I flinch from the tension between them.

"Fuck off, son." Lucian says, shutting the door after sticking his middle finger up at him. Alec shrugs when I give him a look of surprise.

"I'll always be his favorite son-in-law. He caught Markus under the dining room table with his face buried between Isabelle's legs when we were staying with him." He says, opening the driver's door and holding his hand out for my keys. I toss them to him without an argument and take the passenger seat.

"She was hungry, and so was I. How was I supposed to know he was going to wake up early?" Markus complains in the backseat, his arms crossed as he grins.

"Your car is too small," Jared huffs from behind me, his knees pressed to my seat.

"Keep bitching and I'll pull this car over." Alec warns, following the GPS directions to a nearby airport.

"Lucian has a jet prepped and ready." Alec tells me. I nod, staring out the windshield as we speed down the road, zipping through traffic. I was now split between my son and my wife, but it would be over soon. I'd save her or die trying. It feels good to finally have direction, to know where we are going.

"I'm sorry, Aden." Markus reaches forward, squeezing my shoulder and pulling me from my thoughts. I catch his eye in the rearview, brows pinched as I turn to look at him. "I thought I had killed him, this is my screw up."

"He was as good as dead, Markus. He faked his death and vanished off the face of the earth. I failed to protect Nina. This isn't on you." I say, and Alec snorts.

"We can play the blame game or just admit David is fucked up and this is all his fault." Alec shuts us down.

"Agreed, your pity party is just irritating." Jared mutters, and I hold my middle finger above my seat. This was going to be the longest car ride of my damn life. The plane wouldn't be much better.

CHAPTER ELEVEN

Nina

Standing here, naked, as David sits in his chair beneath me was beyond humiliating. It burns me to the core, more than the bleeding cuts across my back. Olivia is still crying in the corner, with Percy doing his best to comfort her. She dropped David's coffee, and he tried to grab her, but I slammed into him and knocked us to the ground. My punishment is to stand here while Grayson draws a blade across my back. I know he is being gentle, just pressing enough to draw blood and leave a stinging trail as I struggle to bite down the screams. It doesn't stop me from imagining sticking that knife into his stomach.

"Enough." David says, waving his hand as he prowls around me. He stands behind me, sighing as he shakes his head.

"Grayson, you did such a lovely job. These shouldn't scar too much." The sound of ice clinking in his glass next to my ear is the only warning I have before he pours his whiskey over my back. I scream, stumbling forward as the burning pain ripples over my fresh cuts.

"Put her outside, she has garden work to do. Don't give either of them gloves." David storms from the room. Olivia shoves past Percy, racing to catch me as I collapse to the floor. She rocks me as I cry in her lap, and Grayson wraps his jacket over my body before picking me up.

"Get off of her!" Olivia screams, her tiny hands slamming to his arms. Grayson lays me on the bed and blows out a breath as he turns to Percy.

"This has to stop, man." Percy mutters.

"Are you stupid? This isn't your business. The boss does what he feels is necessary."

"It feels wrong, Gray." Percy's voice raises when the shower turns on.

"Your job isn't to feel. It's to follow orders and keep your head down." Grayson snaps, storming from the room.

"Fuck," Percy slams his hands to the dresser, and I watch him through puffy eyes until he looks at me.

"I'm so sorry." He whispers, glancing back over his shoulder.

"Protect her. Get her out of here, Percy." My voice is just above a whisper but I know he hears me.

"He'll let her go soon," I know that he doesn't believe the words as they leave his mouth.

"Okay, the tub is ready. Let's get you washed up so we can bandage you." Olivia is trying to sound positive but I can hear the way her voice wavers. I grab Percy by his sleeve as he turns to leave and he stares down at my hand before pulling away to stand with his back to me. Olivia helps me stand, letting me lean on her as we stagger into the bathroom.

My hands are sore, but the clouds were giving us some relief as we worked to plant the dozens of Crown of Thorns and rose bushes David had bought. Percy drops a couple bottles of water between us, and we don't waste any time gulping them down while he stands over us. I notice that he does his best to block the sun from Olivia when it peeks from between clouds while we work. Grayson joins us when we finish digging a hole for a particularly massive Crown of Thorns.

He leans down and plucks the plant up to drop it in the hole, waving Percy off.

"Boss has some paperwork he needs you to take care of." They share a knowing look as Percy sighs, rolling up the sleeves of his shirt as he walks away.

"You could just say he needs to interrogate somebody. Code words aren't necessary for us." I say, as we pack the dirt around the plant. Grayson crosses his arms while watching us but doesn't say a word or offer help as we finish the last row just as the sun begins to drop and our stomachs are rumbling. Percy returns as we are cleaning up with a basket in his hand. He looks overall disheveled but has a smile on his face.

"David is in a meeting, and he instructed me to bring you dinner." Percy sits the basket on the grass, pulling out a blanket to smooth it on the ground. Olivia brushes her hands off, excitedly sitting on the blanket as she smiles brightly at Percy.

"Thank you for thinking of us," she says. Percy clears his throat, trying to avoid Grayson's death stare.

"He'll skin you for this." He warns the blue haired man. Percy shakes his head, giving me a sideways look.

"A man should take care of the woman he fancies." Percy winks at Olivia, and my heart soars when I catch his meaning. He is going to get my sister out of here. Olivia and I sit together, eating in silence as we enjoy the late evening breeze. My mind is racing through the plan I had been working out. Percy will take Olivia, and as soon as she is safe, I'll kill David. I've never taken a life, but I couldn't leave here without doing it.

David won't stop, and my son's life will be in constant danger. I wasn't naive enough to think I can make it out of this alive, but at least

I can do this for my family. For Aden, when he saved me all those years ago. It's my turn to save him.

"You're plotting something," Olivia is smiling, pointing up at the clouds.

"What?"

"Don't look alarmed. Keep smiling and act like we are just watching the clouds. You have a plan, what is it?" She giggles, and the sound is so fake that it makes me laugh. Percy and Grayson frown in our direction but they go back to talking with their heads leaned together.

"Nothing solid yet, but I'll tell you as soon as I come up with something." I take her hand in mine, tilting my head up to soak in the last of the sun's warmth. Grayson checks his phone, motioning for us to get up. We leap to our feet, and I shoulder Olivia behind me.

"Fun is over, boss is coming." He almost seems to hold his breath when David comes storming out. He is stretching his arms above his head, yawning as if he's had an exhausting day. His eyes settle on me, and he holds his hand out. I hesitate, until he turns to Olivia with a sharp grin. I quickly step forward and put my hand in his, gripping tight enough that I hope it hurts. David just laughs, leading me towards the house as he walks away.

"Grayson, I have work to catch up on. You will stay guard in my room until I return, she doesn't leave." David says, kissing the back of my hand with a light bow. "I just didn't want my sweetheart sitting in the sun for too long." His charming manners always catch me off guard, leaving me staring after he walks away.

"Let's go," Grayson grumbles, taking my elbow to push me up the stairs. I wrench my arm from his hold and he rolls his eyes at me before I stomp ahead. I childishly slam the door shut, getting more irritated when it bounces off his palm. He stands there with a grin, winking at me as he steps into the room.

"Percy told me that there's a little bird who wants to spread her wings." He steps forward, kicking the door shut behind him. I take a step back, eyes flicking around the room as I search for anything to defend myself with. Damn it, Percy. I'll rip your smurf ass hair out for this.

CHAPTER TWELVE

Aden

I slam the nozzle back into the pump with more force than necessary and Alec watches me carefully. I don't say a word before making my way into the gas station. The best part of being out so late at night was the lack of people. A bored cashier barely looks up at me as I walk to the coolers, grabbing a soda for me and tossing one to Alec.

"You know my favorite soda, how touching." His voice is dry and I roll my eyes at him.

"You're buying," I shove my soda into his hand as we walk towards the counter. The man in front of us drops an armful of snacks and drinks on the counter, one falls off and I lunge forward to catch it. The plastic flexes in my grip as my knuckles whiten when I stare at the painfully familiar label.

It's Nina's favorite.

"That was an impressive catch, buddy." He takes it back with a nod of his head.

"Couldn't decide which one you twanted?" Alec raises a brow, looking over the collection of junk food and different drinks. The man laughs, rubbing the back of his neck as the cashier quickly rings up his order.

"Friends gave me vague snacks they wanted, I figured I would go the safe route and get a little of everything." He shakes his head, handing them a wad of cash before he walks out, whistling to himself. Something inside of me urges me to follow him, but all I have to go on is a stupid bottle of tea. I stand near the doors, watching him slide into the passenger seat of a small sporty red car.

"Spit it out," Alec says, tossing my drink to me as we leave. I shake my head, deciding against leading us on a wild goose chase when it was just a man buying tea.

"Didn't like his blue hair?" Alec asks, and I roll my eyes as we climb back into the car. Alec pulls out his phone, reading off a message on his screen.

"Markus said he has something, and sent us GPS coordinates." I can feel my energy twisting and curling inside of me. We are getting closer, I can feel it. But I won't be able to take a real breath until Nina is back in my arms again. The wind blows through my open window, carrying the smell of the ocean with it as I watch every face that we pass. More than once my mind focuses on a flash of dark hair, but each time I know it isn't her.

The little park we pull into is just like any other, and nothing jumps out at me. Except for Jared's massive figure smoking a cigarette as he looms over a familiar looking woman. Her white hair is twisted in a bun as she perches her hands on her hips, a matching look of rage on both of their faces.

"You can't just fucking stowaway on a plane, Lunatic." Jared snaps, throwing his hands up.

"Well I can and I did. So suck it up, because I am here to help." Luna turns to me, rolling her eyes as if her husband is being unreasonable. I have the patience of a damn saint for not putting my foot up both their back ends as they continue to bicker. Markus is grinning like a fool, sitting on the hood of their SUV with a cigarette hanging off his lip.

"Lover's quarrel, how sweet." He sighs, wagging his eyebrows at Alec who was much less amused.

"Was this the big news?" He asks his brother.

"Nah, I found her in the plane when we landed and helped her hide in the car for funsies. This little sly psychopath has been scouring the internet and hacking into all local security feeds to search for your wife's face." Markus flicks his cigarette butt, sliding off the car as Luna turns to us with an excited bounce in her step.

"Yes," She claps her hands together, giving Jared a snarky look over her shoulder. "I haven't found her anywhere, yet."

"That's the big news? You've got to be shitting me," I want to shout, to break something at how stupid this entire day has been.

"Calm down, crabby pants. Let me talk or I'll shave your eyebrows while you're sleeping, you taint." Luna gives me a look that tells me she isn't screwing around, and I wave a hand for her to continue. "I found David, but just once. On the same day that Nina vanished, he used a bathroom in this super cute little shopping center. The man with him on the other hand pops in pretty frequently. He's been crawling all over this sandy little shithole." She looks down at her nails, glancing at Jared as she waits.

"You are going home," He tells her. Luna looks to me for help, but I hesitate because Jared is right.

"If you're here, then some of my focus will be on protecting you and I'm not sure I can afford the distraction." I admit.

"I've proven myself a thousand times and you still only see me as a hurdle." The pain in her words makes me flinch, but Jared grabs her shoulders and gives her a small shake.

"I can't risk losing you, Lunatic." He snaps, and she reaches forward to cup his face in a way that makes me feel as if we're intruding.

"We could continue this senseless disagreement, or just accept the help and look at what Luna has found." Alec speaks up, always the voice of reason. Luna goes to the car, pulling out her laptop as she opens multiple files.

"Here's the guy we saw lurking around David," She begins.

"Fuck," I curse. "Shit," Alec says at the same time. The blue haired son of a bitch from the gas station. My instincts were screaming at me, and I ignored them.

"You know this guy?" Luna asks.

"We saw him at the gas station." Alec says, scrubbing a hand over his face as he turns away to control his temper. But I'm beyond control. I slam my foot into the side of the car, denting the passenger door as I let out a cry of rage. Luna quickly grabs her laptop before it falls off the car and Jared grabs my shoulder, stopping me from making an even bigger scene.

"What's up, princess? Wanna buy him dinner before you eye fuck him?" Markus calls to a man that openly stares while jogging past us. He stumbles, righting himself as he runs faster and Luna grins.

"Come on now, don't be shy. He's a very gentle lover." She shakes her head, high fiving Markus while Alec works his jaw to the point he looks in physical pain.

"I've felt that rage, the helplessness. Don't let it cloud your judgment." Jared tells me, turning to Luna with a shake of his head. "Stop harassing strangers." He scoops her up, stomping back to the car with her thrown over his shoulder.

"I'll send you all the information I found on him. Dude's name is Percival, so he's probably a complete douchebag." She calls back to me before Jared tosses her into the backseat and shuts the door behind them. Markus frowns, giving Alec a pleading look.

"Don't make me get in there with them. They're definitely doing immoral stuff, and I don't want them to corrupt my innocence"

Markus inches towards the driver's door of our car. Alec rolls his eyes, stomping towards the other vehicle without saying a word.

"Your innocence?" I ask, raising a brow. Markus smirks as we both get into the car.

"I'll have you know that I am a lady, thank you very much." Markus says in a high pitched tone, syncing his phone to the car's GPS. I already miss Alec's aloof personality, as Markus starts singing off key to the music that blasts through the speakers. If Nina ever doubts my love for her, I haven't swung on Markus in a few hours. That should say something.

CHAPTER THIRTEEN

Nina

Grayson looks sick as he stands in the doorway and watches David lose his mind. David wrenches the dresser, ripping drawers loose as he throws them across the room. I stay where I am, cowering against the wall with a hand cupped over the bleeding wound on my face. My eyes flick to the knife that is lying near my feet, my blood still smeared over the glinting blade. Grayson moves before I can, kicking the weapon behind him and into the hallway. When I look up at him, he shakes his head once, warning me that it would be futile.

David turns to face me, pointing a shaking finger in my face as he storms closer. I lean backwards but he grabs my throat, lifting me until my feet dangle and my toes scrape across the hardwood floor.

"You ungrateful bitch. I give you a home, food and clothes on your back. Night after night you keep trying to turn me away and I'm sick of being a nice guy. You'll submit to me or I'll fuck your sister while you watch." He spits the words in my face as I scrabble against his grip, my vision blurring as my lungs beg me for air.

"Submit," He hisses the word, throwing me and bashing my body against the wall. My head slams backwards so hard that I see stars and a sickly cry wheezes from me as I suck in air. My tears burn while they stream down my face, and I watch as they mix with my blood to drip crimson spots onto the floor between my hands. I bow my head, touching my forehead to the floor and a sob shakes my entire body.

"Get her fucking cleaned up before I come back." David shoves me out of his way with his foot as he leaves, slamming the door behind him. Grayson is suddenly next to me, trying to help me up. My face is slack and I allow myself to sink into a safe place within me. Somewhere that monster will never touch.

"You told him you would never give yourself to him, Nina. What were you thinking?" Grayson asks, opening the frequently used first aid kit on the bed next to where I'm sitting. I give him a cold stare, forcing him to look into my eyes.

"Don't look at me like that." He grunts, smearing antiseptic across my face.

"You are no better than him. He's going to rape me, while you stand on the other side of the door and let him." I say, my voice flat. He flinches, looking away as he calms his breathing.

"I don't like this any more than you do. David knows where my fucking daughter is. If I stand against him, he'll hurt her, or worse, Nina. I can't do anything to put her in danger." His voice is a low shout, and I can see the genuine fear in his eyes. "I want to help you, but please understand when I say that I can't let what's happening to you happen to her."

This man, with piercings through his eyebrow, a skull tattooed on his head and knuckles covered in more scars than skin is afraid. He isn't afraid of David, he's afraid of what he would do to somebody he loves. To his daughter. I reach out, putting my hand in his as he stares at them. "Gabriella has already lost enough, when her mother died. Biologically I'm her uncle, but I adopted her when she was just a baby. I can't let her suffer because of my stupid decisions." He shakes his head.

"You should go get her and run as far as you can."

"I can't do that, he will find us. David has eyes and ears everywhere, he can reach you no matter where you hide. If I kill him, he has loyalists that would do the job for him and hunt us down. This is the only way I can protect her." He shakes his head, turning to leave. "You remind me of her. My sister Carmen. She was kind, and fiercely protective of me. A little bossy, too." I can hear the strain in his voice.

"I forgive you, Gray." I say. Grayson stops with his hand on the door. His shoulders slump before he walks out and leaves me sitting alone. The lock slips into place and all I can do is pray that Percy sticks to his word and gets my sister far away from here tonight. Grayson is right, whoever kills David is as good as dead.

My head is still throbbing as I lay in the bed, pulling the blankets around me as if they will protect me from the monsters just as they did when I was just a little girl. But these blankets aren't a magical shield, I'm not safely tucked in and the monster isn't under my bed.

"I'm glad you've decided to show a little gratitude." David's voice is low as he clicks the lights off, shutting the door gently. I keep my eyes closed as I hear him emptying his pockets and taking his shirt off.

"Open those pretty eyes, Nina." He tries to sound seductive, but his voice makes my stomach churn. The blankets are ripped away from me and he's not impressed by the leggings and oversized shirt I am sleeping in. Grayson had brought it in, sneaking it alongside the sickly sheer lingerie set that David sent for me.

"Whose shirt is this? You let my men fuck you and think you can just parade around and rub my face in it?" He asks, acting as if I've done something absolutely deplorable. But I bite my tongue, climbing out of bed with slow movements as I peel the clothing off. Shame ripples through me as I kneel for him, wearing the lacy bra and thong, keeping my head tilted downwards. David hums his approval and holds his hand down for me to take. I place my palm in his, letting him pull me to my feet.

He sighs with mock sadness, his fingertips ghosting across my abdomen.

"Don't worry, I'll find a way for them to fix this. You'll be beautiful again." He nods and points towards the foot of the bed, telling me where to stand. I brace myself, imagining that when I open my eyes, it'll be Aden waiting in the bed for me. But no matter how hard my mind tries, I can't conjure it.

When I look around the room, my eyes land on the nightstand and a rush of energy comes alive in my body. I'm no longer a doll, plastic and emotionless. David lays back in bed, squinting at me with suspicion. He realizes what I'm staring at when I dive towards it, but he's too late. My hands wrap around the cold metal, lifting the heavy gun as I point it at his chest. David throws his hands up, uncertainty flashing through his eyes as he watches me.

"You're gonna hurt yourself, put that fucking thing down." He yells, but help won't get here in time. He locked the door when he came in.

"My husband taught me how to shoot. Aden gave me power, so that I would never have to cower beneath scum like you." My lip trembles, but my voice is steady as I turn off the safety. David swallows hard, shaking his head.

"No baby, he tainted you. A woman like you shouldn't have to do this, Nina. Your place is not behind a gun, it's behind a man who will protect you and give you everything you need." he tries to reason, slowly getting to his feet as I back away.

"My place is at Aden's side, or six feet under the ground. I will never stand behind you, David." I peer down the gun, taking a steadying breath. But my body is frozen. My finger won't move, and my hands begin shaking. David sighs, shaking his head as he steps closer.

"You're not a killer, baby. Give me the gun and we can talk this out. I promise that I won't be angry." He says, holding his hand out as he steps closer. My finger flexes, pulling the trigger as I imagine that same hand reaching towards Leo.

The gun clicks, and we both stare at it with a mix of confusion and horror.

"You would have fucking shot me," David says, slapping it from my hands. "It wasn't loaded, you stupid bitch." He grips the back of my hair, wrenching my head sideways as he unlocks the door. I scream and kick, desperate to break free as he drags me towards the stairs. Grayson is watching us with wide eyes as I'm paraded in front of his men.

"Bring Olivia to me, now." He tells one of his men.

"No!" I screech, fighting against him as I feel my hair being ripped from the scalp. I twist, raking my nails down his face as I unleash a feral scream. David jerks me backwards, throwing me at Graysons feet. He catches me, keeping my head from hitting the ground and cushioning my landing.

"Hold the bitch down and make her watch," He tells Grayson, turning away. He nods, but doesn't follow his orders. Grayson carefully helps me stand, wrapping an arm around my chest just tight enough to keep from mauling David.

"I'll give you my jacket when he's occupied, just try to hold still." The words are a whisper in my ear and Grayson gives me a pleading look when I turn to see his face. The man David sent to bring my sister back comes running down the stairs with a red face. And he comes back alone.

"She's gone, sir." He says. David turns on me with a snarl, ripping Grayson's gun from his waistband to press it against my skull. Olivia is gone, she's free. I can't stop the smile that curls my lips as David leers at me. Grayson has become wary, and I can see him struggling on what to do.

"You have nothing to use that can make me bend to your will," I smirk, leaning back against Grayson as I let my eyes slide close. David slams the butt of the gun against my face, lifting it to continue as I fight to turn away, but Grayson wrenches me back.

"Take a breath, boss. We can get her back." He says. David stops, enraged eyes not quite focusing as he waits for him to speak.

"Percy was with her, I can track his phone. We'll bring them both back." He says in a placating tone.

"Don't do this, Gray." I begin twisting in his arms, struggling to get my hands loose so I can do *something*. David nods, pacing the floor in front of us in nothing but his boxers, scraping the gun against his head as he walks. I find myself praying for it to go off, and when Grayson leans close to speak, I slam my head backwards into his face.

"Damn it, Nina," He groans, using his free hand to cup his bloody nose. I lean back, spitting in his face and pissing him off more. I don't want to hear his voice, his half assed attempts at empathy. Part of me knows that what he's doing is for the sake of his family, but I have to protect mine.

CHAPTER FOURTEEN

Aden

We found the son of a bitch. Markus was tailing behind a small red car the moment Luna flagged them on a security camera and we had stayed right on him. I want to blow out his tire, wreck his car and bring him to the brink of death until he tells us everything. Jared has a better plan, we were following him and waiting for him to lead us to wherever David was slinking around. My hands flex, my knuckles popping as I struggled to sit still as we tailed the car through the dark, winding roads.

"He's heading towards the docks," Markus peers back at the GPS, looking back up at the car ahead of us. Sure enough, we pull into the massive parking lot close to the marina and keep our distance until he parks.

"He's got a woman with him," Markus says, his voice coming from next to me and the earpiece I clip onto my right ear.

"Is it Nina?" Luna's voice is hopeful, and I can't help but feel the same way. When the woman steps out of the car and pulls a hood over her head, I climb from the car and rush towards them.

"It's Olivia, Nina's sister." I say, pulling my gun out as I creep closer. Markus catches me, nodding his head to a darkened spot in the direction their heading and I nod once. We split up, circling them as we rush to cut him off.

"You just need to trust me," The man says, putting his arm around her shoulders. Olivia has her arms wrapped tightly around herself as she shakes her head and tries to plant her feet.

"I can't just let her die, not like this and not for me." Olivia cries. Markus slips out in front of them, whistling as he strolls casually between cars.

"Lovely weather, ain't it?" He stops, tilting his head as he looks them over. "Have we met before? You look awfully familiar, miss." He taps his chin. The man steps in front of Olivia, pulling her behind him protectively.

"Anything we can help you with, buddy?"

"Not my favorite," Markus wrinkles his nose.

"Pardon?" The man asks, obviously confused by Markus.

"I prefer being called kitten, or maybe even Sir Sex God, if you're feeling bold. Buddy just feels so bland, don't you agree?" Markus Steps closer, finally egging him on to draw his gun.

"I don't know what you're on, but we're done here. Let's just go our separate ways." I slip up behind them, slapping my hand over Olivia's mouth and dragging her backwards and she screams and tries to cling to him.

"We can go our own ways once you tell me where your boss lives, Percival." I tell the man, pointing my gun at him. He spins to face me, realizing Markus has also pulled a gun on him.

"She's got nothing to do with this. Let her go." His voice is full of concern as he holds his hand in the air. Markus steps forward and easily plucks the gun from his hand.

"Percy," Olivia's voice breaks as I pull my hand away from her face.

"You're safe, Liv. We'll get you back home." I say, and recognition lights up her eyes.

"Aden?" She asks, throwing her arms around my neck. I hold her tight, not taking my eyes off of Percy while I rub her back and try to comfort her.

"He's helping me, please don't shoot him," She steps away, wiping her tears as she gets closer to Percy. Of all the things I wasn't expecting, this tops the list.

"Well, smurfy here is a good boy. Color me shocked." Markus snorts, not lowering his gun.

"You want to fucking live? Tell me where my goddamn wife is," I step closer, pointing the gun at his head.

"I'm gonna reach for my phone, I can pull up the coordinates from there." Percy says, slowly pulling his phone out. He taps on the screen while I watch, finally showing me an address in his history. I have to close my eyes as I pull a deep breath through my nose. We drove down this road, and most likely went right past this exact house. Olivia grabs my arm, her grip surprisingly strong as I look into eyes the same shade as Nina's.

"She did everything to get me out of there. Nina protected me, no matter what horrible things he did to her. She saved me." I know what she's saying. Nina sacrificed herself and as soon as they realize their leverage is gone, she is gonna pay for it.

"Gonna share what you know, or just leave us with blue balls? You should also know, I can't access his phone because it's being tracked. My guess, limp dick wants his people back." Luna's voice crackles through my earpiece and I roll my eyes.

"I'm sending the address now, meet us there." I say, smashing the phone beneath my shoe before throwing it across the parking lot. Percy drops his hands, his jaw dropping open.

"What the hell, I'm not your enemy, dude." He pouts, resting his arm around Olivia's shoulder as she leans into him.

"I don't want you on our side if you're too stupid to realize you're being tracked. Get on the ferry, and get the fuck out of here. You get on a plane and David is gonna have somebody waiting for you when you land. Don't make me regret this." I pick up his gun, slamming it to his chest before running towards my car. Nina will kick my ass for leaving her sister in the hands of a stranger, but I don't have a minute to waste.

"Race you there," Jared chuckles into my earpiece and I grin, excited as I slam the pedal to the floor while Markus barely has time to shut the door.

"You're crazy, and if I'm saying it, then you're batshit level." He yawns, completely unaffected by my reckless driving. I can hear him and Alec chattering through the headphones, but their words don't pierce the haze I've sunk into. I knew that David was hurting her, but I didn't stop to think about the extent that creature was willing to go. When we get close, I slow the car down to draw less attention but it drives me crazy to do it. By the time we finally park outside, my entire body is twitching.

"I have an idea," Luna repeats, finally catching my attention through my earpiece. "I'll ditch my shoes, rub sand all over me and go right up to the door and say I'm lost and need help." There's silence for a split second before Alec sighs.

"You're staying in the car, and that's enough from you." Jared snarls, and I see an interior light come to life down the street as Jared climbs out of his car and rips his earbud out. He approaches our car, leaning through my open window.

"We don't have time to fuck around, we need to go in there." I check my gun, making sure it's fully loaded as Jared watches the house with suspicion.

"Damn it, get your ass back here." Alec hisses, and Markus and I look up in time to see Luna shoot across the road. Jared still hasn't noticed and I take a deep breath, sharing a look with Markus. Forming a plan has just become 'follow the big angry motherfucker into the chaos'. Jared looks up in time to see her shimmering hair slip through the front gate.

"Luna," He roars, charging after my sister. Markus grins as we follow them and somehow I find comfort that I'm with the most unhinged one out of all of us.

CHAPTER FIFTEEN

Aden

Luna walks right up to the door and knocks on it. We all stay in the shadows, doing our best to hold back Jared as he watches every movement without taking a single breath. I am going to shake the shit out of her when we get out of this mess. After a few moments, the door swings open and the porch light flicks on to illuminate the man. He's almost the same height as her, with a stocky build and he's wearing a plain t-shirt and shorts as he stares down his nose at her.

"Hi, I am super sorry for pestering you so late but I fell asleep on the beach, and somebody must have snatched up my stuff. So I am super lost and scared." She lays it on thick, even stepping closer to the light as she glances over her shoulder as if she's afraid of what is lurking in darkness.

"Why'd you pick this house? There's a gate that specifically says no trespassing." The man mutters, eyeing her suspiciously.

"I figured a nice house like this would have a nice family inside willing to help a girl out." She shrugs, leaning towards him. I can see the moment he stops believing her. When the hard lines settle between his brow and his hand disappears behind him.

"Damn, I thought that was convincing." She shakes her head, ducking low to the ground. Jared rushes forward, raising his gun and shooting the man down. We all funnel through the double doors, weapons raised as we pick off everyone with a weapon within a matter of minutes. There were only half a dozen waiting behind the door, and I listen carefully for any movement in the house. Alarms are blaring in my head that something is wrong as we spread out and begin clearing room after room.

Luna returns from the kitchen brandishing a couple kitchen knives with one between her teeth as she wiggles her brows. A slight scuff behind me is all the warning I get before she raises one of the knives and I lean sideways, the blade sailing past my head to sink into a woman's face.

She falls to the ground, her blood pooling around her red hair as I blow out a breath.

"Where the fuck are they?" I whisper. Luna shakes her head as she listens, edging towards the stairs. I push in front of her, glaring when she bares her teeth at me like a wild animal. A creek from the hallway keeps me tense as I rush upstairs and catch sight of a man diving into a side room.

When I race after him, he plasters himself to the wall and raises his hands. He's unarmed and still looks pretty young, twenty at best with his long blonde hair and spattering of facial hair.

"Where is David? What did he do with Nina?" I ask, staring down at him as he slides down the wall and begins praying. I'd roll my eyes if I wasn't already fighting off a headache from the adrenaline.

"Each time I have to ask is another hole in your ballsack, so cough up some answers." Luna points a knife dangerously close to the man's jewels and even I flinch from her threat. The guy shakes his head, and starts crying. Luna gives me a horrified look before turning back to him.

"David will kill me, please," He whimpers.

"Tell us where he is, you get to live and possibly make little babies who will cry less than you, and David dies. Now that's what we call a win, my boy." She taps her knife on his leg, nearly making the poor man screech.

"He left. He took her with him, but I don't know where they're headed." He cowers, wrapping his arms over his head as we share a look. Luna steps past me as I turn away and point the gun behind me, pulling the trigger. I hear the thud of his lifeless body when it hits the ground and Luna gives me a disapproving frown.

"He could have given David the heads up that we're onto him. I won't show mercy until I can paint these walls with the blood of every man who stood by while he touched what is mine." I brush past her, racing for the stairs. I was following my own twisted need for revenge, and direct orders from Lucian himself.

Luna pulls her phone out, pacing as she taps the screen so hard that I expect the glass to break under her thumbs. We all gather in the hallway, patiently waiting until her head snaps up and her face splits in a smile.

"He owns a fucking boat," she says, and I wave my hands while waiting for her to explain. "They're most likely headed for it right now. There is a boat dock just down the road, let's get a move on." Luna takes off with me hot on her heels. By the time we race down the dock, it's too late. I can see the massive boat floating in the distance, just a few lights sparkling in the darkness.

"Shit, now what?" Alec mutters, looking around at the boats floating next to the dock.

"Anyone ever hot wire a boat before?" I ask, and Markus lets out a sadistic chuckle.

"Which one tickles your fancy, brother?" he holds his hands out as if it matters. I jog down the dock, stopping at the one that looks the fastest.

"Oh flashy, daddy likes." Markus leaps onto it with a chuckle, ripping the cover off as he gets to work. I keep my eyes locked on the boat, refusing to lose sight when we are so close. The dark waves lap beneath my feet, and I think back to when she taught me how to swim, laughing as I floundered around the pool. Little did she know, I was a lifeguard once upon a time and could have swam laps around her. But I would have done anything to be close to her, just as I will now.

The boat rips to life, the engine sputtering as it roars and shifts in the water. We all climb in, Jared waving his hands as he shoos Markus away from the controls.

"Last time we were in a boat and you drove, I had to fish everyone out of the water. Get back," He grumbles, and Markus throws his hands up in defeat. I lean against the edge and hold my hand out, catching the cool water as it sprays around the boat. Alec bumps his shoulder against mine, nodding towards the larger watercraft.

"We will catch up to them, and you'll have the rest of your life to make this up to her." He says, staring at the moon that reflects on the surface. "I remember that feeling. As if I had failed Isabelle, then we found her just to have you and her father rip her away from us again."

"If I knew then what I do now, Alec," I shake my head, not sure what else to say. He shrugs, giving me a crooked smirk.

"You're one of us now. We'll finish this together, as brothers." He says, clapping a hand on my back. My chest tightens from his words, and my confidence grows with all of them backing me. We will do this.

Chapter Sixteen

Nina

My stomach lurches again as I lean forward, trying desperately to fight back the nausea that consumes me. Grayson holds out a bottle of water, but I swat it from his hand and turn away. The world under my feet tilts again and I press my forehead to the filthy floor. Grayson sits back on his heels and tries to pull me up by my arm, but I'm in no mood to cooperate. The hatch above the stairs squeaks as it opens and Grayson curses, yanking the gag around my neck upwards and shoving it between my teeth.

He should be grateful that I don't sink my teeth into his fingers. David stands in front of me, shaking his head with mock sympathy.

"I forgot how much you hate being on the water, my delicate little thing. Just be grateful you're still on the boat instead of in the ocean." He sighs, patting my face too hard. I turn away from the sting, reminding myself that Olivia is okay and that I can endure whatever happens from this point on.

"We have some guests following us. I think your little whore of a sister called in the fucking calvary." David's hand strikes across my face before I can flinch away, the burning sting ignites over my cheek as I fall sideways.

Grayson catches me, gritting his teeth as I stay limp in his arms. David's words are slow to register past the throbbing in my head, and I can vaguely hear Grayson telling me to keep my head down and stay quiet. Laughter bubbles through the cloth in my mouth as I lock eyes with David.

He stares down at me as if I've grown a second head and I curl my lips into a grin. He reaches out and wrenches the fabric from between my teeth and I swallow hard, trying to soothe my dry mouth.

"Want to share with me what is so fucking funny?" He asks.

"Nina," Grayson warns.

"My husband is going to cut you into pieces so small, minnows won't have to chew you." My voice breaks and my lips cracks and I smile wider. I can see the redness crawl along his veiny, thick neck as his flash with murderous rage. David brings his foot back, kicking towards my body but never makes contact.

Grayson lurches backwards, standing suddenly as he pulls me with him. David stumbles sideways as he's caught off guard and his rage turns to confusion.

"Who the fuck do you think you are interfering like that?" David shouts, throwing his hands up.

"If they come for Nina and you beat her to death, you've got no bargaining chip, boss. What if it is her husband? You didn't fare well against them the last time you had a run in." Grayson speaks softly, using a placating tone. David shakes his head, reaching up to tug his hair as he walks. I can see the strands between his fingers when he pulls them away and races towards the stairs with two other men hot on his heels.

The hatch slams shut behind him, the sound making my ears ache as we shift on the ocean. Grayson blows out a breath, straightening me as he looks at my cheek.

"You're either brave, or reckless. I haven't decided which one." Grayson shakes his head, but I can see the empathy in his eyes. I step away from him, looking around the bright white room. The small kitchen below deck was disorienting but it was better than the bedroom I was in before. I peered at the countertop that had a row of drawers below it. One of them had to have something inside of it worth using as a weapon. Grayson leaned into my line of sight, raising a brow.

"Bringing a butter knife to a gunfight? Reckless it is." He shakes his head as if I'm the problem. I keep my mouth shut, leaning back against the wall as I struggle to listen. The sound of the engine drowns out everything else, but even if it's my imagination, I hear the faint rumble in the distance. Grayson leans next to me, crossing his arms and he tips his chin towards the hatch.

"Your husband is gonna slaughter every one of us, ain't he?" Grayson asks.

"Yes, he is."

"Good," His one word catches me off guard and I twist to stare at him. "Each and every one of us has done something unforgivable, or stood aside while David did. Wipe us all out, it'll be a better world." He says, smiling as if he is relieved by the idea of it.

"You did what you had to for your daughter."

"I did what I did because I don't have a fucking soul, sweetheart. It's not any deeper than that."

"You're a good person," I say. Grayson scoffs as he walks past me to sit down at the bench and table that is bolted to the wall. He waves a hand, motioning to the seat across from him.

"Come sit before you fall on your face, not that it can look much worse. When shit starts to pop off, I want you under this table. I won't let anything happen to you, Nina." He says, and I sink down on the bench. My mind races as I try to come up with a way that we make it out of this alive, so that he can return to the daughter that he sacrificed so much for.

I betrayed my husband to protect our son, and I couldn't judge him for doing the same. A gunshot echoes above us, the sound vibrating through the metal as we both stare at the hatch. Grayson pulls out a knife, snatching my hands in his as he swipes the blade between my wrists. The ties that bound me snap apart and he pats my hand, turning the knife to hand it to me with the hilt first.

I hold it tightly, crouching beneath the table as Grayson stands in front of me. My hands shake as I wait, listening to the sound of shouts above us of gunshots and feet slamming across the floors. Another strong wave rocks us as the door slams open and Grayson struggles to keep his footing.

"Get her the fuck up and give her to me!" David sounds frantic as he thunders towards us. Grayson's gun clicks as he points it at David.

"You're not going to hurt her anymore, David. You've lost, it's time to give up." He tells him, his voice calm but stern. David laughs, pointing his gun at me while he steps closer.

"You are pathetic, Grayson. You let easy pussy convince you to betray your own daughter? Get a fucking grip. If I die, so does your little girl. Go ahead and pull that trigger and show me what kind of man you are." David steps closer, leveling his gun at me.

The shot erupts just as another wave rocks us, the sound piercing my ears as I fall backwards with a scream and slam my head against the wall. Black spots blur as warmth spreads over my body and I desperately struggle to open my eyes and pull each breath into my lungs.

CHAPTER SEVENTEEN

Aden

She is here somewhere, and I'm not leaving without Nina in my arms. Markus lunges to the steering, launching us sideways as he spins the watercraft, spraying up a wall of water before speeding around the side of the boat.

"It's now or never, ladies." He smirks to us, smacking up against the side of David's boat and sending all of us to the floor.

"This is why I steer and you sit your ass down," Jared snarls, helping Luna onto his back as he leaps upwards, catching the rings and heaving them onto the deck. I follow after them, hearing Luna and Jared shouting to each other as they rip through the men waiting. Gunshots and the sound of metal pinging fills the night as I stare at the five dead bodies that are bleeding on the deck.

"I got three," Luna pumps her fist excitedly. Jared rolls his eyes, keeping himself low to the ground.

"Don't let your guard down, Lunatic. I'll catch up with you." He mutters. I ignore their banter as Alec nudges me with his elbow, tipping his head towards the captain's area. I nod, leaning next to the door as I reach for the lever and slowly pull, unlatching the door. Once everyone is in place I twist and swing it inwards. Shots ring out, sparking as they bounce against metal and miss each of their targets.

"Where did they find their men, the freakin' cabbage patch?" Luna shouts, her voice loud in the following silence.

"That doesn't even make sense," I grunt, lurching through the doorway. Luna picks up a piece of metal and flicks it, bouncing the piece off my forehead while I glare at her. "Quit screwing around."

A man pokes his head out of the doorway, and Luna raises her hand. She pulls the trigger without blinking or looking away from me, grinning when his body slumps to the ground. I roll my eyes, but a small part of me sings its pride for my little sister and how far she's come. The boat suddenly lurches, rocking all of us. Luna puts the back of her hand to her mouth, her cheeks paling. Jared wraps an arm around her protectively and I tip my head for him to drag her away, before she pukes everywhere.

Alec raises his brow, nodding to tell me he has my back. I dive through the doorway, and slam into a waiting wall of muscle. "Shit," The massive man whips out his gun, but I snap a kick to his wrist and he drops it with a grunt. He yanks my wrist, twisting until agony ripples through my arm and my gun clatters to the ground. I catch sight of Alec wrestling on the ground with an enraged woman straddling his chest.

She is trying to force the serrated blade into his abdomen, putting all of her weight behind the hilt. Alec is holding his own even though she has the upper hand. I don't have time to stare when the giant man grabs the front of my shirt and lifts me off my feet, tossing me as if I weigh nothing. My back hits the wall and I slide down, choking as the air is knocked from my lungs and I feel warmth drip down my chin.

The taste of copper is unmistakable, and he's not done with me yet. I can hear voices below us, and as the boat shifts again, it knocks my opponent off balance. A gunshot rings out from a floor down and the next sound makes my blood turn cold as it rips through my entire soul.

I would recognize her voice anywhere. Nina's scream cuts short and I slam my fists to the ground as if I could rip this metal apart with my bare hands. Leaping to my feet, I rush at the man and slam to his middle, knocking him backwards and tripping him over the dead body of the woman Alec was fighting.

When I land on top of him, I slam my fists into his face, again and again even as his massive hands slump to the floor.

My Nina. Her scream still reverberates in my head, each impact against my knuckles slowly drowns out the sounds around me.

Blood slicks across my hands, each punch slipping over his skin as I let my rage consume me. My anger comes out in snarls until a small hand slaps across my face and bright white hair falls into my vision.

Luna grabs my jaw in a pinching grip, forcing me to look at her as she frowns. "He's dead, Aden. Let's go." She snaps. I rise to my feet slowly, staring at my hands as they shake. The skin is split and raw, covered with another man's blood and my own. Jared runs towards us, waving for us to follow him down a narrow staircase.

"There was a gunshot. We heard a woman scream." Alec explains, and I can feel his eyes on the back of my head. "Nina. It was Nina's scream." I hiss, shoving past everyone to rush for the door.

"Your gun," Alec says, grabbing my shoulder as he shoves it in front of me and I take it without stopping. The door swings open and I don't stop. Even when I come face to face with David.

"Give her back!" I roar, pointing my gun at him. David grins, his hand pressed to the bleeding wound on his side. From the corner of my eye I see *her*. Nina is held by her throat, a gun pressed to her head while she dangles in somebody else's arms. Her beautiful hair is plastered to the side of her face and neck with a thick layer of blood. My eyes lock onto the droplet that falls from her chin down to the floor.

"I'm going to take you apart, David. One fucking piece at a time until you're nothing more than a whimpering bitch, begging for mercy." A cold calm has settled over me, finally seeing her again.

"Nina was on her knees, nothing more than a whimpering bitch. How ironic." He mutters, his disgusting grin getting bigger. "He's baiting you, Aden." Alec says, his foot bumping mine as he steps closer. I know David is just trying to get under my skin, but it's too late. He's been tearing through my flesh from the moment he stole my wife.

The four men around the room are all positioned with their guns leveled at us, not including the one that is holding Nina and the man lying at their feet. Nina groans, the low sound coming from her as she slowly lifts her head. I watch her hand twitch, trying to reach for her head but the man holding her slaps it away.

"Don't fucking touch her!" I roar, stepping towards them.

"He gets any closer, shoot her." David says, watching me with a calculated eye.

"It doesn't have to be this way, David. You won't leave this room alive." Alec tells him. David scoffs, blood dripping from his mouth as he shakes his head.

"Gray?" Nina says, staring at the body at her feet. She tries to lean down, reaching for him with a choked cry. "Grayson, wake up." I can hear her voice breaking as she reaches for him.

"Your little whore really gets around." David sneers, spitting on the motionless body. Nina finally looks up, tears staining her dirty face but I can see it. The bravery in her eyes that he hasn't broken.

"You're pathetic and I pray Aden snaps every bone in your body. I hope I get to watch him as he breaks you." She cries, shaking her head.

"That's my girl," I say, my voice a whisper. Her eyes finally find mine, her lip quivering as a sob wracks her body and she tries to lunge for me. The man holding her slams the barrel of his gun to her head, and it takes every ounce of restraint I have to not kill him. Yet.

"Let her go and you can walk away from this, David. We have an entire fleet of men waiting just beyond these stairs. You kill us and it's over for you no matter what." Alec offers and I open my mouth to argue, but Jared grunts behind me and I snap my jaw shut. I'll agree to anything if I get to hold Nina again, to take her away from this pain.

I can see David considering it, and when two of his men lower their guard to lean towards each other, the boat rocks and I leap into action. I slam into David, knocking him to the ground and wrapping my arm around his throat as he fights me off.

My arm tightens and when the barrel of my gun taps his temple, his entire body locks up and he holds his hands up to stop his men.

"If anything happens to Nina, if he plucks a hair from her head, I'm going to kill you. It'll be slow, and agonizing for you, but I'll enjoy every second. I wonder how long you'd live if I peeled your fucking flesh away from your bones and cover your body with acetone?" I mutter in his ear, tightening my hold until he struggles to breathe. None of us are expecting the man at Nina's feet, Grayson, to leap from the ground.

CHAPTER EIGHTEEN

Aden

Grayson knocks his body against Nina and the man holding her, sending them to the ground and the man's gun flying. Grayson's hood falls away, showing the skull tattooed on the back of his head as he grips the man's head and snaps his neck before anyone can move. He covers Nina with his body, baring his teeth like a feral animal as he looks around at all of us. Blood covers the left side of his face, dripping from his mutilated ear.

A flare of jealousy rips through me. David lets out a shout and rolls, taking me with him as he grabs my gun and tries to wrench it away. My ears pop when another gun fires and I catch Jared using one hand to rag doll a man. The sound of his bones breaking makes my teeth clench, and my hands tighten. David sinks his teeth into my arm as he loosens my grip and I can feel the skin ripping. I slam my fist into his nose, hearing the sound of it cracking brings me a twisted satisfaction. He lets go finally, gasping for air as he chokes on his own blood that leaks from his broken nose.

"Kill them," He shouts, coughing as he slowly gets to his feet, the two of us staring each other down.

"This ends here." I tell him. David smirks, and lunges for me. My head smacks the floor, but I fight past the pain, beyond the blurring in my vision. I slam my palm to his already injured nose, making him roar with pain as he straddles me and swings a fist wildly. Throwing my arms up in time to block, I punch his wounded ribs and he jerks away.

"I'm not done with you," I jump to my feet, bringing my leg back to slam a kick to his side. I don't see the gun in his hands as he crawls away in time. But when he raises it, it isn't at me.

Nina's wide eyes are on me as she mouths the words *'I love you'*, but time seems to slow. I dive onto him, the shot ripping through the air a breath before I drive my knee into his head and rip the gun away. David stops moving, unconscious beneath me as I turn to see the pain in Nina's eyes.

She slams her palms down, putting pressure on the red stain that spreads over the fabric. My feet feel as if they're cemented in place until Jared's anguished cry rips through me.

"Luna!" He drops next to her as Nina does her best to stop the bleeding. I rush to their side, my arm wrapping around Nina as I brush the hair from my sister's face. Her skin is clammy and she reaches out to cup Jared's jaw. "I think I won this time, Biggums. I got more than you." She smiles, but I can see the heavy way her lids droop. Jared nods and for a moment, pride flashes across his face as he cradles her in his lap.

"You sure did, Lunatic. But then you go and pull another stupid stunt and put the two of you in danger." He shakes his head, struggling to keep his composure. "We need to get her out of here, now." Jared doesn't take his eyes off of Luna. Nina slumps against me, struggling to keep pressure. A hand holds out a ripped sheet, nodding for me to take it. I quickly fold it, guiding Nina's hands away as I take over. When I press down, Luna whimpers, burying her face against Jared.

"Be easy, you fucking idiot." He snarls. But the words don't hold any malice. Alec has vanished up the stairs and we all quickly follow Jared as he gathers his wife. Nina wraps her arms around my neck and I rub my face in her hair, breathing her in. I don't think I've ever seen Jared move so fast, until Luna's hand falls away from his back, and her head drops backwards.

"Luna, you better open your damn eyes before I fucking pry them open!" Jared cries, and I shove him forward, pointing to where Alec holds a phone to his ear and shouts into it. A helicopter appears in the distance and Alec shoves his cell into his pocket.

"Just a little longer, Jared. She'll be okay." Alec's voice is steady, but there's uncertainty in his eyes.

"She's not breathing!" He lays her down, clamping his mouth over hers to force her lungs to inflate. Nina is crying silently in my arms as I watch in horror. His massive hands cover her chest, pounding down to make her heart beat. My wife is safe, she's in my arms, and I'm watching my sister die. Grayson stops next to me, tossing David's limp body to the ground. His hands and feet are bound, and I nearly smile seeing the gag shoved into his mouth.

"Grayson helped save me," Nina says and I hold my hand out to shake his. He stares at it, frowning before taking a step back. "I helped torture her." He mutters, the sound of the helicopter nearly taking his words as it lands on the deck. Markus leaps from it, ducking low when he rushes to me as paramedics swarm my sister.

"We can take two," He begins, and Nina points to Jared and Luna. "Take them. I'm okay." She says, her grip tightening on my shirt. Selfishly, I breathe a sigh of relief as I watch Jared follow my sister. We watch in silence, fear burrowed deep.

"If she dies, that entire thing is gonna fall to the earth in a ball of flames." Markus' tone is serious, and I know he's right.

"Remember when he threatened the doctor's life over Luna, and when the doctor tried to kick him out, he bought the damn hospital?" Alec says, shaking his head before he leans against the railing and rubs a hand over his face. Grayson's words sink in and I slowly turn to face him.

"You tortured Nina?" Ice flows through my chest as I speak and Nina sighs.

"David was threatening his daughter. Grayson just did what he had to do and I forgive him." She says, making me pause as I stare down at her with wide eyes. I can see the wounds across her body, the bruising that covers her exposed skin. Her blood is dried and crusted on her cheek. Yet she still has sympathy for somebody that hurt her.

"Keep your fucking pity, Nina. There's no excuse." Grayson snaps at her and she rolls her eyes.

"Watch how you speak to her, or I'll make David look like a fucking teddy bear." I warn him. I find a place to sit and wait for the boat Alec calls for us. I can't stop rubbing my hands over Nina as I convince myself she is really here, and she's alive.

CHAPTER NINETEEN

Nina

Smearing my hand across the glass to clear the fog, I can see Aden's silhouette as he watches my every move. The first thing I wanted when we were home was to see our son, but I had to wash away what I could. Or try to at the very least. Aden hasn't let me out of his sight and I can't be more grateful, even if we've barely spoken. The shampoo slips from my fingers, crashing to the floor and I slam my hands outwards to catch myself as I stagger backwards with a soft cry. Aden slowly opens the door while stripping his clothes off as he climbs in to stand with his chest to my back.

His arms wrap around me, holding my shaking body tight as he hums in my ear. I lean into his touch, finally relaxing after a breath and he leans down, picking up the bottle and gently massages the soap into my scalp. My chest clenches, my heart aching. He can't fix the newly broken pieces of my soul, but I know with time he will help me put them back together. Even if there will always be cracks.

"You're home, Nina," He mutters the words, almost to himself as he guides me to turn and dip my head beneath the water spray. Why do I still feel as if a part of me is trapped in that room, chained down and locked away for good?

"We need to get you checked over, there's a doctor waiting for us downstairs whenever you're ready." He frowns at the loofa in his hand, then back to the wounds that pepper my body. The shallow gashes on my back aren't terrible, but they still sting and burn beneath the water. The entire left side of my face is an array of bruises and split skin, and I know the butterfly stitches Alec helped put on aren't enough to hold the skin together.

"I'm asking, because you can tell me anything." He takes a breath, and my stomach twists when his eyes find mine and he cups my cheek with his hand. "Did he hurt you, or touch, anywhere we can't see?" The question sends a shudder through my body and my eyes slide shut as I drop my forehead to his shoulder. Aden's fingers dig into my hips and he holds me tighter, until I shake my head. His breathing stops and his entire body locks up.

"I'm still going to make him fucking suffer, my heart. I'm going to make him beg you for forgiveness while knowing the only mercy that awaits him is death." The words are dark, animalistic and I take comfort in them. I shouldn't, and the woman I was a month ago would cringe away from the idea.

"I want him to suffer," my voice is steady, and Aden pulls away to hold my face gingerly. His lips curl as he watches me, seeing something in my eyes that makes him happy. "You are so damn strong. Let's go get you bandaged up, I know a little guy who has missed you as much as I did." He says. My sweet little Leo, I rush getting dressed in Aden's oversized black t-shirt and shorts, tolerating him carrying me down the stairs as I favor my sore ankle.

I think he just wants an excuse to touch me, to have his hands on me. The woman waiting in the living room gives me a friendly smile, her eyes raking over and I can see her mentally noting the visible wounds. Her long doctor coat is nearly the same shade as her pale hair, and I recognize her immediately, Dede slaps Aden across the back of his head when he gently sits me on the couch.

"You made her suffer when you should have called me the moment you landed, boy." She chastises, immediately setting out her medical kit as she shoots him a grumpy look. Having been employed privately by the Barone brothers for their entire lives, she never asks questions. But she didn't bite her tongue and I felt a fondness for the woman that has stitched my husband back together more times than I can count.

An hour later with more stitches than I'd like and Dede stands back, eyeing her work. "You poor girls always bear the wounds of your husbands, while they wear matching ones on their hearts. I can't say I envy you." Aden's phone rings and he finally stops pacing long enough to answer it.

"How is she?" He means Luna, his sister that took a bullet for me. "I'll be there in ten," He hangs up, turning to me as he tries to wipe the fear from his face.

"I'm coming with you." I say, turning my back to him as I hobble to the stairs. I can hear Dede laugh when he starts groaning, saying their goodbyes as he chases after me. "She was shot because of me, and she's my family too." I keep my head held high and he sighs, looping his arm around my waist to help me get dressed.

Seeing Jared so distraught almost makes me turn and walk back out. Luna looks exactly as she did last time she was in this hospital, except the burns across her face and neck are pink scars instead of being swathed in thick white bandages. Wires are poking out from beneath the fuzzy blanket Jared tucks around her, again.

"She gets cold easily." He says, his voice low as if she's just sleeping. The steady beep in the corner followed by the hissing of air from the tube in her throat makes my hand tighten around Aden's. He brushes a strand of silver hair from her face, and I notice how tangled it's becoming.

"I need a brush," I say, and Jared digs one out of a bag he must have packed for her. I slide a chair close and sit near her head, gently pulling her hair out to fan the pillow as I carefully brush the silky strands. I can feel her husband's eyes locked onto me and my hands start to shake.

"I'm sorry, Jared. This never should have happened. It should be me." I can't look up. I can't look at him even as his massive frame towers over me. When he sits on his heels, crouching until we are eye level, he reaches forward and flicks my nose. I startle and jerk back, looking at him in shock.

"Luna didn't have a family growing up. We," Jared motions to all of us, waving his hand to encompass the Barone's that aren't here yet, "Are her family. Any one of us would do the same for each other. Would you do it for her?"

"Absolutely." I tilt my chin up, and Jared has the ghost of a smile on his face as he stands. Luna's nurse comes in at that moment with wide eyes and another behind her pushing an ultrasound machine. Jared stands straight and Aden comes behind me as we watch her nervously tap on the screen of her tablet.

"Out with it," Jared snarls. The nurse looks at us and motions for the door. "You might want to step out, so we can discuss some things."

"That's my sister," Aden says, and Jared crosses his arm with a brow raised. She sighs, looking at the screen as she speaks.

"Her hormone levels are concerning. They should be trending upwards and while they aren't dropping, they're not where we would like them to be. We're just gonna check on the ultrasound." She says. Jared has nearly become a statue, his face frozen between irritation and fear.

"How far along is she?" I ask him. I wonder if he's heard me after a few minutes pass until he finally takes a deep breath, glancing at me. "Sixteen weeks," The words leave him in a rush, and I stumble over to hug him. Jared awkwardly pats my head, stepping away as he drops onto the sofa and watches the nurses prepare the machine and gel.

"Luna's pregnant?" Aden asks, finally catching on. Jared just nods with his interlaced fingers pressed tight to his chin. "Jared, hold her hand." I whisper and he looks up at me, suddenly a lost and broken boy. "Luna needs you to hold her hand while they check the baby." I gently say. He takes my abandoned seat, laying his head on her chest as he cradles her hand. Too much time passes as they rub the wand over her stomach, twisting and turning.

Then we hear it.

The steady and quick thrum of a beating heart. Jared's shoulders tremble as buries his face in her neck and Aden claps a hand onto his shoulder. His eyes are locked on the screen, wide and full of conflicted happiness nearly identical to when we were carrying Leo.

"Holy shit, my little sister is going to be a mother." The wonder and joy in his voice makes my throat constrict. I slip from the room, silently closing the door behind me as I lean against the wall with my head bowed and my hands braced on my legs. Luna is fighting for her life, and their child's life, while I stand here and struggle to hold back tears.

Chapter Twenty

Nina

A soft whimper from the busy hallway makes me whip my head around as I look for the source. I would know that cry anywhere. I see Aden's father Vincent smiling as he and Isabelle hurry towards me. Isablle is grinning with a carseat in her hands and tears in her eyes.

My baby. There was a time that I wasn't sure if I would ever see him again, and I can hear him crying louder when I rush to meet them. Isabelle wraps one arm around me as I grab the seat, crying as I look at Leo. He whimpers, yawning while stretching his neck to stare at me. I fumble with the buckles until Isabelle reaches forward to unclip him and I pull him to my arms.

He squeals, grunting as I rub my face against his chubby little neck and breathe him in. A large, warm hand cups the back of my neck and pulls me against a broad chest. Aden lifts me off my feet, startling me as I cradle Leo and look up. Content is the best way to describe his expression.

"My legs aren't broken." I smirk. Aden huffs, barely glancing at me until we step into a dark room and he kicks the door shut behind us. "Aden?"

"I want to be alone with my family." He lays on the hospital bed, Leo between us as we curl our bodies around him. Aden props his head on his hand, looking between us. Leo clings to Aden's hand as he taps his tummy, tickling him as he grins down at our baby.

"I love you both so much." My voice feels loud in the quiet room. The way that Aden's gaze burns through me takes my breath away as I wait for him to say something, anything. After the silence stretches to a point I can't stand, he blows out a breath and shakes his head.

"I'm afraid that you'll disappear when I close my eyes, Nina. What you went through happened because I failed you all those years ago. Seeing Luna like that, I feel so damn wrong for being relieved that you're okay." I can see it now, the fear mixed with waves of guilt in his eyes. I reach for him, my mouth opening to tell him it's not his fault when his pocket buzzes and interrupts us. He groans when answering it, sitting up as he answers with his name.

He snorts a laugh and I watch as his face splits into a malicious grin. "Tell them I am always up to hearing them out, but they'll be getting their precious son back in pieces." He hangs up and shakes his head while staring down at the screen.

"What was that about?"

"David's parents apparently got wind that we have their shitty kid. They want to offer us something they don't think we can refuse. As if anything like that exists." He scrapes his fingers through my hair, gently tipping my head back to press a kiss to my forehead.

"He's still alive?" Fear ripples through me and my hand flies to Leo's chest as he yawns sleepily on the bed next to me. I can see the rage flicker behind Aden's eyes but he shakes his head and grips my hair just enough to keep my attention.

"Nina, he won't touch you ever again. Do you hear me? I couldn't let him get off so easily, and there is something I need from him before his miserable existence finally comes to an end at my hand." The confidence in his voice should be enough, but every wound across my body throbs in time with my racing heartbeat as a reminder of what that monster can do. A soft knock at the door draws Aden away when the light flicks on. Isabelle is standing in the doorway with her arms hugged tightly around her body.

"Nina," She breathes out, stepping closer. Aden scoops up Leo, turning his back as he gives us a minute. The second I open my arms, she rushes forward and hugs me so tightly it takes my breath away and tears sting in my eyes.

"Easy, she's hurt." Aden taps Isabelle's arms and she pulls back with a laugh, brushing a hand over her shining eyes. "She's fucking alive, Aden. I'm so proud of all of you for bringing them both home in one piece." She says, and I clear my throat to swallow the lump that forms.

Except I'm not in one piece, and neither is Olivia. Percy hasn't left her side from what I've heard, but she won't get out of bed unless he drags her. She won't even let our parents visit her and I'm trying to be understanding and patient, but I'm ready to go break her door down so I can see her myself.

Markus is lurking in the doorway, watching us closely. I can see Aden's father behind him, but he doesn't look at me before turning and walking out. The tapping of his cane follows as he leaves, and my stomach sinks more with every step. He blames me for this, I'm sure of it and I don't blame him.

We all file out, squeezing back into Luna's room. I'm grateful Jared made sure she was put into one of the larger suites, and I sit on the edge of her bed as Aden hands Leo back to me.

"Your nephew misses you, and they grow so quickly that you can't afford to miss a moment. You'll understand when your little one gets here, Luna. I hope they have your strength, because there were a hundred times before that you could have given up but you didn't. So don't give up now, okay?" I clench my eyes shut, gripping her hand tightly in mine.

Tears fall, dark spots spreading over Leo's blanket as he sleeps.

A flutter.

Nothing more than a twitch, but I hold my breath nonetheless. "Luna?" my voice is a croak as I lean forward, staring at her closed eyes.

Jared stands so suddenly that his chair flies backwards, crashing to the ground. In one long stride he is kneeling next to the bed, cradling Luna's other hand in his own.

"She squeezed my hand!" He roars the words, and Leo kicks up a fit at the loud sounds. Her eyes flicker back and forth behind closed lids, but we all see it and when she squeezes Jared's hand once again, he loses all composure.

His head drops to her shoulder as his large body covers hers. "Live, Lunatic. Live for me." He says, and suddenly the room is swarmed by doctors and nurses that force everyone out except for Jared.

Leo is crying loudly as I bounce him, all of us in shock until Isabelle dives into Alec's arms. I lean against Aden, my energy nearly draining as relief rushes through me.

"Looks like the big guy won't be tearing this building down with his bare hands today after all." Markus grins. Isabelle stands between them, laughing as she rubs at her puffy eyes. I notice that both of the men are touching her stomach, speaking to each other as if it's just instinct.

If there is justice, if there is any higher power, Luna will pull through this just fine. We all deserve a happy ending.

Chapter Twenty-One

Aden

She has changed. Nobody could blame her, after the Hell she endured, but Nina was different. I had never seen her lose her temper this way. The physical therapist was staring daggers at me, but I was just a spectator here. The vase pieces scattered across the ground surrounded by the wilting flowers weren't actually thrown *at* him, so I don't know why he was looking for backup. Nina is panting, sweat dripping from her brow as she stares at her feet.

"Your distance is improving, so obviously you're making progress." I say, peering at her over my mug as I sip my coffee. The look she gives mc would make most wither, but it just makes my cock hard.

Her eyes flick to the obvious tent in the front of my flannel lounge pants as I grin. The physical therapist averts his gaze blowing out a breath.

"I told you that regaining full use of your arm would take time. You sustained serious damage to the muscle and tendons. That isn't something that will magically repair itself." Roger mutters, and Nina growls.

She actually growls and I can't stop my laughter. Her anger turns to me, but I watch her clutch her trembling arm with her stronger one and it cuts me short. "Leo needs you to not give up, my heart." I remind her. This only pisses her off more as she grabs the weight, gripping it tight and I raise a brow. I was expecting it to sail across the room, but she grips it firmly, puffing a breath in and out as she holds her arm out.

"That's my girl," I say, winking at her as I walk out of the room, brushing past her physical therapist. "Learn to duck, bud. If she wanted to hit you, she would've." I smirk when he takes a step further away from her. Before I make it to the couch, my phone vibrates and I roll my eyes when I see Percy's name on the screen.

"Olivia is asking to see her sister." He says. That makes my eyebrows shoot upwards, Olivia has been refusing to see anyone for the last week that they've been home. "I'm bringing her to your house, she needs to get out."

"I'll let Nina know." I say, hanging up. He still pisses me off, I don't give a shit if he helped her sister. Percy and Grayson both stood aside while my wife was beaten, assaulted and could have been so much worse.

A sharp sting rips through my hand as water and porcelain splatter to the ground. Droplets of crimson follow as I stare at the mug crushed in my palm. My hand was already covered in scars, and most of them were my fault.

"Aden?" Nina says behind me and I turn to catch her frowning at the mess. She takes my hand in hers, sighing as she picks the small bits left behind out of the wound. The scrapes are minor, and I tug my hand away from her.

"Let's get dressed, Olivia and her nuisance are coming to visit." It takes Nina a moment to register what I'm saying and she smiles before giving me a roll of her eyes.

"Percy is a good person, you promised to give him a chance and be nice." She reminds me.

"I take it back." I mutter, following her up the stairs. Her hips sway, testing the bounds of my self control as I watch her ass climb the stairs ahead of me. This pent up energy is getting ready to explode, but I just clench my bleeding fist, letting the pain distract me.

As if the dull ache alone could be enough. Something other than my pain helped when the woman I love and cherish flinches away from a hand reaching towards her. I was going to pay my friend a visit, and Percy was going to help me.

I turn to one of my most trusted hired guards, Anne. Nina is comfortable around her, and the two get along well. "You stay with her, don't let them out of your sight. Understood?" I ask. She nods once, standing at the front of the room with her back to the wall.

Standing with Nina safely behind me and my gun in hand, I open the door to let Percy and Olivia in. She's clinging tightly to his shirt and his arm is wrapped protectively around her as they step inside. I roll my eyes when Nina shoves past to grab her sister in a hug and Percy tries to hold onto Olivia. The sisters walk away, their heads bent together while holding on for dear life.

Percy and I stare at each other, his eyes flicking to the gun in my palm that I'm not bothering to hide. His blue hair is lighter, as if it's faded since we saw him that day at the docks.

"Are you going to kill me?"

"Maybe."

"Swear to me that you will protect Olivia, make sure she keeps going to therapy and don't let her out of your fucking sight." He crosses his arms, and I roll my eyes, motioning for him to step inside.

I pull out my phone, calling in a few guards that Nina has nicknamed the babysitters.

The two men and one woman take their places by the front door, one near the back and another stands behind the women as Olivia watches with wide eyes. Nina glares at me but I just wink, nodding my head towards the back door.

"I need Percy to help me with something, we are within ear shot. If you try to leave or shake your guards, they're under strict orders to cuff you and call me. Don't push me today, my heart." I grip Nina by her chin as we pass, kissing the corner of her mouth and relishing in the moment when she doesn't flinch.

"Don't kill him, Aden." Olivia says, reaching over the back of the couch to grip Percy's sleeve. He chuckles, gently prying her hand off and brushing his knuckles over her cheek before following me.

"So you rescued the princess, swept her away from the big bad man and took advantage of her vulnerability?" I ask him when we trudge through the back yard stopping at the large shed where I press my thumb to the scanner while typing a code in with my free hand.

"It's no like that," His voice raises in defense before I turn to quirk a brow at him. "Her therapist said she did start forming a trauma bond with me, but nothing has happened between us."

"I don't fucking believe you." I say, walking into the mostly empty shed and wrenching up the carpet to open the hidden hatch.

"Then don't believe me, but it's true. I sleep on the floor next to her bed because she wakes up screaming. When she showers, I stand with my back to her so that she can see me but I don't even peek at her. Physically she's perfectly fine, but until she's healed inside I won't fucking touch her." He grips my shoulder, stopping me when we get to the bottom of the stairs. I swat his hand away, shaking my head as I flick the switch that brightens the hallway.

"Keep your fucking chivalry. Nina may forgive you, she may even feel gratitude for you saving her sister, but I don't. You stood aside while my wife was beaten, and she is the only reason you and Grayson are still alive." I snarl, turning my back on him once again.

"Grayson is still alive?" I can hear the excitement in his voice and it only grates on my nerves as I clench my jaw. At the end of the hallway is a door with locks along the side that take me minutes to open.

"What is so important you have all this security?" He mutters. I can't stop the twisted grin when the door opens, and the man in front of me cowers as much as he can while tied to the chair.

The two guards across from him make quick exits, and the stench hits me. Percy gags from the smell of David sitting in his own feces, but I only smile bigger. His face is swollen, the bruises slowly yellowing at the edge with blood crusted to his face and bare chest. The gag tied around his mouth quiets his threats, the empty ones that wheeze from his lungs.

"I thought he was dead," David's eyes flick to Percy when he speaks and rage gives him empty bravery when I yank his gag away.

"You worthless fucking scum. Your buddy Grayson fucked my girl so you just had to take her sister and run off, screwing everything up." He spits the words. My fist connects with his weak jaw, the bone makes a sick crack beneath my knuckles as his head whips sideways. The inhuman scream that he lets out nearly makes me feel guilty.

Until Nina's bruised and battered body flashes through my mind.

I walk around behind him, pointing to the table next to Percy. He glances down, drumming his fingers until he stops on the bolt cutters, his gaze sliding to David. The ties hold steady as he thrashes in the chair as Percy steps closer, and his boyish face has become menacing in the low light.

"You threatened Olivia, you made her sister do horrific things to protect her." His voice is frigid, and even I'm impressed by him as David closes his eyes and begins praying.

"You're going to watch," I whisper, wrenching his arm around to slam it onto the table. David shakes his head, struggling like a wounded and cornered animal. But he's weak and I've been pushed beyond my limit.

Percy lines up the sharp end around David's finger, and I nod my head once. "For my sister." My words are drowned out by his scream, followed by David dry heaving and sobbing when we strap his arm back into place.

Chapter Twenty-Two

Nina

My sister is snoring on my lap, her chest rising and falling as I drag my fingers through her hair and bite my lip to stop a laugh when Leo's grunted snores match her own. Anne is still standing, her face a hard mask as I stare. I offer her a place to sit, but she adamantly refuses, reminding me of her orders from Aden. Every person beneath his command follows him without an ounce of doubt because of how much they respect him.

Anne stands straighter, which I didn't even think was possible, as Aden and Percy's voices reach us. A deep chuckle catches me off guard when I see them with similar crooked smiles before they see me. Percy's smile drops as he brushes a hand through his blue hair and frowns.

"Nina, I just wanted to say that I'm sorry. I should have stepped up and done something to protect you," I wave my hand, cutting off his words.

"David would have killed you on the spot, then who would have saved Olivia? David would have still been using her to force me to do whatever he asked. I owe you my life for saving hers." I say, smiling down at my sister as she drools on my leggings with her mouth hanging open.

"You don't owe anyone a damn thing." Aden mutters, kissing the top of my head and then Leo's. He stares at my sister with wide eyes when she snores, then looks at Percy.

"You look like shit because this human freight train keeps you up all night?" He says as if answering his own question and Percy gives him the middle finger before sitting next to me and pulling Olivia's feet into his lap. Aden bristles at how close we are and I pat the cushion on my left for him to sit.

"You helped Grayson find his daughter," it's a statement from Percy and Aden sighs. "Nina wouldn't let me kill him, and the idiot wasn't armed when he told Markus to just put him out of his misery. Markus was more than happy to try." Aden shrugs. I haven't told Aden that Gray and his little girl are going to be staying with us. Or that Isabelle offered him a job working under the Barone's, and there's no time like the present.

"We have a few spare rooms, one is yours for the night." My husband says and Percy tenses, used to Aden's hostility but not his kindness.

"Not the room with two beds," I cough, letting my hair fall forward to cover my face. Aden slowly sits forward, pinching my chin between his thumb and finger to force my eyes to meet his. "You're hiding something," his lip curls as he waits for me to find my words. "Spit it out, Nina."

"Isabelle got Gray a job working for the Barone's. Also, he and his daughter are going to stay here until they find a place of their own." I spit the words out and bite my lip, waiting for his reaction.

Betrayal flashes across his face and he stands abruptly.

"Fuck," Percy hisses, jumping to hold his hands up. "You can't let what he said get to you, dude. It's not like that, Grayson isn't interested in Nina. He never was. You'll understand when you meet

Gabriella." Aden locks his fingers behind his head as he takes a deep breath.

"Can't let what who said get to you?" I ask.

"It's late, Anne can show you to your rooms. She will stand guard, call for her if you need anything." Aden says, turning on his heels and leaving us as he scoops up Leo and takes him. Percy looks at me with pity and it only adds to my growing bad mood.

"David planted a seed of doubt that you and Grayson may have had a few interactions, if you catch my drift." Percy says, carefully sliding his arms under Olivia to lift her and Anne steps in front of them to show them the way to their room.

Leo is sleeping soundly in his crib, and I have to remind myself not to storm into our room and slam the door off the wall. But the temptation is stronger with every step, and I want to lose control. I want to burn away all of this rage, the helplessness and frustration that is building low in my body. Aden is sitting on the bed with his back to me, and my control slips. I reach down to grab my slipper, throwing it at him. Aden leans to the side, the shoe whipping past his head as I follow with the second one.

Aden turns, catching it and tossing it aside without looking at me. I climb into the bed, standing over him as I grip my pillow and whack him with it. Aden looks at me like I've lost my mind. Maybe I have. He doesn't flinch as I slam the puffy weapon to his chest, but when I try to swing a second time, he catches it and yanks. Losing my balance sends me falling into him and Aden easily catches me, crushing my body to his with my knees on the bed.

"Knock it off, Nina." He murmurs, but there's no anger in his voice. I choose the mature road, snaking my hands through his hair and wrenching his head back. He bares his teeth, hissing as he head snaps forward to glare at me.

"You're being a brat and I don't have the patience for it tonight."

"How dare you believe I would ever let another man touch me?" My voice cracks, and Aden's brow furrows as he watches tears fill my eyes.

"Gabriella is biologically Grayson's niece, but he's raised her as his own since her mother died. I remind him of his sister, Aden. That's why he felt protective of me." His expression softens as he leans his forehead against mine, brushing my tears away with his thumbs.

"You're making it difficult for me to hate him," He sighs and I giggle, leaning back to look at him. Stress and exhaustion has deepened the lines on his face and I skim my hands over them, as if I can smooth away the damage inside and out. Aden shivers, catching my hand as I scrape my nails over the back of his neck.

"We need to sleep." Aden pulls away, putting a gentle kiss to each hand before he steps back. The denial stings as I sit back on my heels, watching him get our pajamas from the closet. If he keeps treating me like a piece of cracked glass, I was going to shatter in his palms. I race across the room, shedding my clothes as I turn off the light and hurry back to the bed.

When he returns, he stops at the foot of the bed and his eyes rake across my skin, leaving a heated path in their wake as they settle between my spread legs. The clothes fall from his hands as he watches my hands slide down my body, over the bruises hidden in our dark room. The only light comes from the glittering fairy lights above our bed and I get to watch his face morph into desire.

His entire body is locked tight, as if he has stopped breathing and turned into a statue.

"Nina," The harsh whisper makes me shiver as my fingers skim over my heated skin as he watches me circle my clit in slow and lazy strokes. When I whimper his name, his control shatters and falls to the floor next to his clothes as he tears them from his body.

Aden grips my wrists, pinning them to the bed above my head as his hot, minty breath fans over my neck. Gentle caressing kisses press to my chest, along my neck and over my jaw. The contrast between his tight grip and hard length that presses into my stomach makes it difficult for me to focus.

"If I hurt you anywhere, if I grab you too tight or anything, you have to swear that you'll tell me." Aden's need to protect me is charming, usually. But right now, I don't want him to be charming. I want him to erase my old bruises with ones from his hand. I want him to steal the air from my lungs, to clamp his teeth dangerously close to my pulse until his teeth mark my skin.

"Aden?" I pant, "Shut up and just fuck me," I barely get the words out when his mouth crushes to mine, his tongue swirling against mine as his hand curls between my thighs, flicking over my clit.

He steals my moans, swallowing the sound as his fingers curl inside of me. It feels incredible, but I want so much more. Aden leans backwards and I reach between us, stroking his thick length as I show him what I want. The empty feeling when he pulls away is suddenly replaced by his head as he slowly pushes inside of me. My back bows, pressing our chests together as he taunts me, sliding inside inch by inch.

Once he's fully inside of me, Aden pins me in place with his hips. I'm desperate for any movement or friction as I squirm beneath him, but Aden grins before nipping at my neck.

"This is torture," I whimper. His deep laugh rumbles through me, sending a pulse between my legs as he grips my hip, digging his fingers in.

"Torture is being married to a woman as beautiful as you, and resisting the urge to fuck you in every room." He thrusts once, rocking my entire body, "To bend you to my will, knowing you'll never break." Another thrust that takes my breath away. "To know that you only kneel for me in these moments, and that I bow to you, my queen." My heart races as Aden slams his hips to mine, our bodies colliding in the silence of the room.

His tender words are a contrast to the harsh way he holds me, his teeth skimming along my throat and a hand tangled in my hair to wrench my hair as he flips me to my knees. Aden slams himself inside of me and reaches around to swirl his fingers around my clit at a dizzying pace. The pressure swells, threatening to stall my heart until it bursts and floods my veins. I cry out his name as he wraps an arm around my waist to hold me up as pleasure steals my senses.

Listening to him moan my name as his thrusts become erratic, his grip over my body tightening until he slams himself into me one last time with my name on his lips.

"You are my paradise, Nina." He buries his face in my neck, holding me tight as if I'm the most precious thing in the world.

"You are my home." I say, yawning as he tucks the blanket around us.

Nina

Olivia's pink cheeks were the first giveaway, the second is the way Percy and her keep sharing stolen glances and smiles. She avoids looking me in the eye as Aden saunters into the room, grabbing the front of my robe to yank me against his chest. He tilts his head, crushing our mouths together and delving his tongue past my lips while I cling to his shoulders for dear life.

"We heard plenty last night, you don't have to show us too." Percy grumbles, turning on the stool to lean his back against the island while Olivia buries her face in her hands.

Aden flicks an irritated look in their direction before brushing his thumb over my lip and winking. "I've grown tired of houseguests. Percy is leaving today." He says, pouring each of us a cup of coffee while I shamelessly watch his bare back. The muscles flex as he stretches, his cocky smirk thrown over his shoulder lets me know he's doing it on purpose.

"Olivia wanted to ask if we could stay a few more days. She's worried you'll snap Grayson's neck in his sleep." Percy snorts and Olivia swats his shoulder with the back of her hand. "It's not that I think you're jealous, Aden. I just think that Gray can push buttons." She gives an awkward smile as Aden sits on a stool, pulling me into his lap to rest his chin on my shoulder.

"I won't kill him in his sleep." Aden sighs, and I see them both visibly relax. "I'm an honorable man, I'll make sure he sees me coming." Well, at least he's honest. He sips his coffee and Percy chokes out a laugh. I roll my eyes at my sister, shaking my head. Aden's hand slips beneath my robe, his fingers dancing over the front of my silk shorts.

The island counter covers us, but it doesn't hide the way my face burns when his fingers dig into the fabric.

"We should be hearing back soon from our friends about the gift we sent them yesterday," Aden smirks at Percy, his fingers hooking beneath the edge of my shorts. We both hold our breath when he touches my bare skin and desire crawls along my spine. I can feel the heat of his breath on my neck when he laughs, slowly sipping his coffee as his fingertips drag through the slick that gathers between my clenched thighs. It doesn't take him more than a gentle squeeze to spread my thighs and I bury my face in my arms on the counter when he finds my clit.

"Nina, are you okay?" Concern in Olivia's voice makes me feel guilty for a split second before the pressure begins building as Aden uses his free hand to massage my neck.

"It was a late night for us, some nights Leo fights against sleep." He lies so easily, and Percy's laugh makes me glance up.

"Yeah, that was definitely the baby that was screaming last night." He grins when Olivia jams her elbow into his ribs and I wish the floor would open up to swallow me up. Aden's fingers plunge inside of me curling in a way that makes my entire body tense at the rush of growing pleasure.

"I'm going to go get dressed, Percy packed us an overnight bag just in case." Olivia smiles at him as he stands and holds his hand out for her to take. Neither of us make a sound as they head up the stairs, and Aden flicks his hand, dismissing the guards in the room as he puts me onto my shaking legs.

I don't have time to think as he spins and lifts me, planting my ass on the counter.

"What are you doing?" I hiss, cheeks burning at the idea of being caught when he takes his seat again and hooks my right knee over his shoulder.

"I'm going to enjoy a breakfast fit for a fucking king," He hums, pulling my shorts off and throwing them to the floor. Aden's hot breath over my bare pussy makes me lay back and cover my mouth. He doesn't bother to start gently, immediately sucking against the sensitive spot that has my body arching off the cold stone.

My breath becomes erratic, panted moans falling from my lips as I try desperately to stay quiet when he stops the assault on my clit, plunging his tongue inside of me in the next moment.

"Aden," I can't stop the sound when he uses his thumb to apply pressure and circle at the right pace that has my eyes heel digging into his back as I desperately pull him closer. His fingers replace his tongue and Aden catches my eye. He makes a show of slowly licking his lips and groaning with a look of a man in pure ecstasy.

"I've never tasted anything better than your pussy," he wraps his lips around my clit, and it shatters my world. The sensations send me careening over the edge of pleasure as my hand tangles in his hair, my hips riding his face along with the waves of my climax.

"Such a beautiful sight, my wife flushed with pleasure and her taste on my tongue." He sighs, sucking his fingers as his head tips back and eyes slide close. That sight alone is enough to melt me, if I had any bones left to melt.

"Are you banging in the kitchen? Get a room," Percy taunts, their door slamming shut again. Embarrassment makes my face burn red and Aden helps me sit up, his lip curling in irritation.

"We have a room, and we have an entire fucking house. I'll bend my wife over every piece of furniture, including your bed." I clap my hand over Aden's mouth, shaking my head and laughing as his eyes crinkle in a smile as he picks me up. He grabs my shorts while I wrap my legs around his waist and my arms around his neck. I feel like today is going to be a beautiful day as he carries me to our room.

I was so fucking wrong. My stomach churns violently as I stare at the note hand delivered to our front gate. David's mother begging Aden for mercy, as I stare through the two way mirror to lock eyes with the monster himself. He wasn't so scary, filthy and crying in the chair he is chained to.

I have to fight the bile that threatens to spill, again, as Aden pours salt in the gaping wound on David's leg. When I caught him and Percy reading a letter and snatched it from their hands, this isn't at all the trouble I imagined they were causing. Aden warned me I shouldn't be here but I was determined to see him pay for what he'd done. My heart is screaming that this is brutal, inhumane and sick beyond words. I should stop them.

I don't.

I don't stop them when Aden pulls Davd's eyelid out to snip the thin flesh in half with scissors, but I do throw up over the floor. Aden tosses his gloves to the floor and races to my side to help me with a gentleness that was so opposing to his actions seconds ago, I question how this is the same man. Olivia wasn't cowering though. She marches in, grabs a scalpel and plunges it into his thigh with a sneer I have never seen before.

Olivia is watching intently next to me again, and she clutches my shoulder to get my attention.

"He deserves this," she smiles.

"Nobody deserves this. It's torture." I shake my head, having had enough. When I storm from the room and limp for the stairs, Aden calls after me. But I have to get out, get to fresh air that isn't filled with David crying for his mother. Or him spilling every secret his family has. Their plans to kill Isabelle's father to take over his territory was shocking, but now, Aden is after as much information as he could carve from the poor bastard.

Olivia hooks her arm in mine as I walk past the house, heading straight for our cars. "I need to remind myself of why he doesn't deserve my pity. I need to see her." I say softly. Olivia understands immediately and hurries along.

"Ma'am, Aden doesn't want you leaving without a guard." Anne says, keeping pace with us while her eyes constantly scan the area.

"Then you can drive us to the hospital. Send a car to pick up Grayson and his daughter Gabriella at the airport, please." I ask her, climbing into the passenger seat of the black SUV without another guard.

Olivia scrambles into the back and Anne takes the driver's seat, weary as she starts the engine. Aden's look of rage fills the rearview mirror as I roll down my window, tossing my cell phone out to the grass as we leave.

Chapter Twenty-Four

Aden

She is going to make me rip my hair out if she keeps pulling stunts like this instead of using her words like an adult. Percy nods to a spot of blood on the front of my shirt and I frown, realizing the irony of my thoughts. I shouldn't have let her come out here, to see this. Nina has never been cruel. She doesn't have the same dark streak as most of us. It's one of the reasons I love her so much, for her bright and kind heart. Anne is going to get her ass handed to her if she doesn't slow the fuck down, weaving through traffic with my wife in the front seat.

"Having a nanny on speed dial is necessary in our world, aint it?" Percy snorts next to me, his posture relaxed as hums to song playing through the speakers of my car. I snort, but don't say a word as we follow the familiar vehicle into the parking lot of the hospital, and my anxiety raises a few notches.

"Olivia told me about your sister. I'm so sorry." He says.

"Sorry for what? She isn't fucking dying." I snap and he holds his hands up defensively.

"Easy killer. I'm saying that I'm sorry because she was hurt protecting Nina. I can't imagine the guilt and the relief you must have been warring with at that moment." He shrugs as we climb from the car and his words make me pause for a breath before I catch Nina's angry glare.

"I don't need a babysitter and a stalker," She shouts across the parking garage, her voice amplified as I walk towards her. "Grayson needs somebody to pick them up at the airport." She speaks to Anne.

"I'll go," Olivia offers and Percy stands behind her with a hand on her shoulder.

"Anne, don't leave Olivia's side. Fuck this up and you're as good as dead." I don't bother watching them climb into the SUV and leave. Nina's eyes widen as she realizes I'm backing her to a corner. I can see the idea form as her eyes flick around the area, and she tilts her body, giving away each thought.

"Don't you dare run from me ever again, Nina. When I catch you, I'll put you over my knee and print that pretty little ass with my hand. If that's not enough, I'll fuck you over the hood of my car until you're a dripping mess and you're begging to come while wrapped around my cock. I'll leave you there, shaking and needy, the same way you leave me everytime you're gone from my sight." I snarl the words more harshly than I intend to, and her eyes widen.

The sound of her feet slamming to the pavement as she sprints away from me makes my cock ache painfully as I watch. This woman is going to be the death of me. My large strides eat the distance between us in moments as I grip her by the hair, wrenching her body to twist and face me. I smother her cry of surprise with my mouth, swallowing the pretty little sounds she makes as I press her body against the cold concrete pillar. When we finally pull away, we're both breathing hard and she bites her lip, her brows scrunched.

"Your words, my heart. Use them." I remind her.

"What you're doing to David is wrong." The words send a flash of shock through me, but I don't react as I let her continue. "He's a monster but that doesn't mean we should be one as well. I don't want him to live, kill him but make it quick." She pleads. I nod once, but it isn't up to me anymore.

"Markus and Alec are coming to ask him a few questions. When they're done, I'll kill him myself." She frowns, probably realizing that what I've done is going to seem tame compared to those brothers when Isabelle and her father's life are at risk.

"But why here?" I ask. She looks away, and guilt warps her expression.

"I thought that maybe seeing Luna would make me angry again. That it would take away the sympathy I felt for that monster."

"Oh, my sweet Nina." I sigh.

"I'm sorry," the words are a whisper from her and I cup her face, tilting her head to look up at me. "Do not apologize for the kindness in your heart." I kiss her forehead. Nina nods as she takes my hand and starts to lead us towards the door but I wrench her arm, pulling her back to me.

"Bend over, Nina." My voice is low and she whips her head up to give me a look of doubt.

"Absolutely not. You aren't going to spank me here like a damn child." The shock in her voice doesn't make me budge as I drag her towards our car. "Aden, you better not!" She shouts. I guide her in front of me, making her face the car as she yanks and curses me under her breath. Splaying her palms on the car, I look around to make sure we are still alone as I pull her pants down.

Nina sucks a breath through her teeth, dropping her forehead to the hood of the car. Seeing her perky ass makes me want to fuck her right here and now, but I'm a man of my word. My palm strikes the soft skin, making her hands curl into fists, but she doesn't stand when I brush my knuckles over the skin as it reddens.

"One for every step you took away from me should suffice." I say aloud, and she jerks her head to stare at me over her shoulder and I grin down, striking her ass again. This time she whimpers a moan, hiding her face against the crook of her arm.

Jared greets us in the doorway of Luna's room, and the dark circles under his eyes are worse today. Luna is still laying in the bed, to some it would appear she was just sleeping. I sure as Hell convinced myself of it nearly every day I came to see her.

Jared drops back to his chair next to Luna and cradles her hand in his. "Go get something to eat and then shower. If she wakes up and sees you like this, Luna might just faint or swing on you." I try to reason with him. He just grunts, finally caving as Nina tries to push him towards the door. He motions to the chair, "Take my seat."

Nina's face reddens and I can't stop the smirk from curling my lips.

"I'd rather stand, but thank you." She shifts, a slight cringe on her face as she tries to look away. Jared gives us an odd look, before realization dawns.

"Fucking perverts." He mutters.

"Luna told me about your mask and the woods. Don't kink shame." Nina points her finger at Jared and he shoves past me with an eye roll. But he doesn't make it out the door when I grab his arm and jerk him back.

"First you tell me to leave, then you won't let me out? I'm in no mood for your fucking games." Jared snaps, pulling away from my grip.

"You should know better than to poke that bear." Her voice is strained, and the scratchy cough makes me wince as I stare in shock. Jared doesn't move. I can see him pleading with me that he wasn't hearing things, his eyes wide. I nod once and he spins, nearly crashing to the hospital bed as Nina scrambles out of his way.

Luna grins as he clutches her face, tears in his eyes. "Hey there, grumpy. You must be tired of being stuck in hospitals with me." She tries again to clear her throat, and Jared grabs up a glass of water so quickly that it sloshes to the floor. Nina buries her face in my shirt as I run my fingers through her hair.

"My entire body is so stiff. How long was I out?" She asks, finally noticing us in the background. Her hand flies to her head as she scrunches her brow. Her face changes as a flood of memories hit her, and her hand drops to her stomach. The fear in her eyes as she stares at Jared nearly breaks me but he covers her hands with his and smiles. "Our baby is okay, you're both okay." He says, leaning his forehead against her.

"You saved my life, Luna. I can never tell you enough what you mean to me." Nina sniffles and squeezes in to hug Luna. Jared doesn't budge and I can't blame him. "I owe you my life, Luna. But if you ever do some stupid shit like that again, I'm going to throttle you." I warn her and she lifts her shaking hand, sticking her middle finger up at me.

CHAPTER TWENTY-FIVE

Nina

My mind is still accepting the relief and happiness from knowing that Luna is okay. She is going to come home as soon as the doctors clear her the next day. Jared warned all of us to stay far away for the next few days and I understand. I wasn't sure Isabelle gave a shit what the big grump demands, considering the glob of jello she flung at his head when he dropped that news.

"You're a million miles away." Aden whispered, tucking a strand of hair behind my ear as we step through the front door. Before I can open my mouth to say a word, a large hand wraps around my shoulder and yanks me away.

"Percy told me you want your poor husband to show mercy for that cock sucker you've got locked in the shed. What the fuck are you thinking, you bull headed woman?" Grayson rumbles, rubbing his knuckles against my head until the friction hurts. I slap at him, catching his cheek as he releases me to cross his arms and stare me down. Aden is stunned, watching the interaction. Just as I expect him to go for Graysons throat, he cracks a small smile.

"We finally have somebody else with some damn sense under our roof." He reaches out to shake Graysons hand, but when they make contact, Grayson winces. "Don't even think about hurting my wife ever again, or you'll be down there next to your old boss. Understand me?" Grayson gives a sharp nod, not breaking eye contact until Aden releases him.

Olivia walks into the room with a little girl in her arms, her round face lighting up when she sees Grayson.

"Papa!" She yells, wriggling free and racing for him. Grayson scoops her up, grinning as he throws her into the air.

"Gabby, these are daddy's friends that I told you about. They're letting us stay here for a little while." Gabby looks at us with wide brown eyes, and Grayson brushes her long dark hair out of her face. I hold my hand out, smiling softly when I get close.

"Well it is an honor to meet you, Miss Gabby. I'm Nina." I say. She looks at her father, uncertain of the strangers she's facing. Grayson smiles and takes my hand first, then motions for her. She places her little hand in mine and a bright smile breaks across her face as she dives into me.

"Aunt Olivia is your favorite, don't forget who does the funny voices." Olivia pouts and Percy rolls his eyes, rocking Leo. I raise a brow and he shrugs, "Nanny had to take off." He explains. Olivia gives him a pointed frown.

"He hasn't sat him down since we got back from the airport four hours ago." She says "Snitch." Percy sneers, rocking Leo when he yawns and grunts. Grayson smiles at Olivia, and I notice the way his eyes linger on her. The blush that crawls up her neck tells me she notices it, too. That will be a problem one day, but I'm too tired to put much thought into it as Gabby lays her head on my shoulder with a big yawn.

"Did the two of you get settled in?" Aden asks Grayson. He rubs the back of his neck and looks uncomfortable as he glances between us.

"I don't know how I'll be able to repay you for all of this. You gave me back the one thing in this world I had prayed for. Inviting us to stay in your home, the clothes, and the bed is just so much." He shakes his head. Aden rolls his eyes and waves a hand.

"Just be ready to work tomorrow." He says.

"I haven't found a sitter for Gabby yet." Grayson frowns.

"I'll watch her." Olivia and I say at the same time, smiling at eachother. After we have all said our goodnights, Aden and I take Leo to our room. It's still early enough that we sit in bed, watching Leo try to balance on his bottom, but he ends up flopping onto his tummy with a giggle anyway.

"What did Grayson mean by the clothes and bed?" I ask Aden. He shrugs, but I jab a finger to his ribs and squint at him until he sighs and leans back against the pillows.

"He hurt you, and dammit Nina, I want to snap his neck with my bare fucking hands each time I see him. But in the end, he protected you. He was willing to die to save you and as a father, part of me can see why he did what he did. Somehow, my heart, you forgave him. So I'll tolerate him." He says, rubbing a hand over his tired face.

"Percy told me that Grayson and his daughter were coming with the clothes on their backs. I asked him and Olivia to order them each enough clothes to hold them over, and Gabby needed her own princess bed. They deserve a fresh start, that little girl deserves it." He says. My hand clutches the front of my nightgown as I blink away tears. The man before me, willing to put aside his own aching heart, was the same one who had David pleading for his life. I reach for his hand, taking it in mine as I wait for him to look at me.

"I may be your heart, but you are my home Aden." I say, kissing him gently at first. His hand fists in my hair as his lips devour me, searing every inch of my body and soul as he steals my breath.

Leo sneezes, drawing us apart as we both breath hard, our foreheads pressed together.

"No one will ever take you from me again, Nina. Do you hear me?" He asks and I nod, kissing him gently. "Except your son, who needs a diaper change." I giggle as he sits up with a sigh.

"You should feel special, I don't do well with sharing. Just ask your aunt Luna, she almost lost a finger for taking my crayons when we were kids. In my defense, it had the sharpener in it." He smirks at me over his shoulder as he scoops our son into his arms. Watching him sway as he walks, whispering to our grinning baby, makes my heart thud even harder inside my chest.

I would sacrifice everything for him. For them. His phone buzzes on the bed and I check the screen, the message makes my stomach curl. The way it did before our family was nearly ripped to shreds when this entire disaster began.

A message from an unknown number flashes, bright like a warning of what was coming.

"Nina?" Aden says, but I can't look away as my mouth dries and I struggle to swallow. "Talk to me, sweetheart." He hurries next to me, his hand catching my jaw to force my eyes to his. I don't have to look at the screen when I speak, the words burned to my eyes.

"Our patience has run to its limit. You will all pay with your lives and land." I mutter, turning his phone so that he can see the screen. A series of photos follow the message, one of Jared and Luna kissing in her hospital room. Another of me holding Gabby. The last one is Isabelle as she straddles Markus and uses her mouth on Alec, the picture taken through a window of their intimate moment.

"Isabelle is going to go nuclear," Aden says, his footsteps muffled as he begins pacing. "Markus is going to want it framed on his wall and

Alec is going to print it out to carry it in his pocket, the fucking pervs."
He snorts.

"How can you be joking right now? Those are all from today, Aden." My voice rises but I can't dial back the panic as it grips my throat. He stops, raising a brow at me as his lips curl into a devious smile.

"Because this is exactly what we wanted all along. His entire family is going to pay for what their threats and the sins of the son that they helped cover up. That beast beneath the shed brutally beat every woman he ever touched. His parents bailed him out and buried it each and every time. His brother hurts children, Nina. Children. That entire family will be wiped from this earth before I take my last breath." He turns away, answering his phone. I can hear Luna shrieking in the background, her curses jumbling together into one long word. "*I'lllfuckingcutthatpervertedlittlebitchtwithmytoenails.*"

"Toenails?" Aden says, looking at me as I just shake my head.

"We're going to put an end to this. Get on with it before Luna burns the hospital to the ground, our insurance doesn't cover arson." Jared grumbles, before the sound of something breaking makes him sigh and the phone call ends. Before he can take a step, it rings again and he pinches the bridge of his nose.

"They sent it to all of you?" I ask. He answers, dropping the phone to the bed between us after setting it to the speaker.

"Isabelle is in the yard threatening every guard with a knife." I can hear the amusement in Alec's voice.

"What she will do to you is fucking cuddles compared to when I shove my boot down your throat and watch you fucking choke." Markus roars, and even I flinch. Alec's laugh is dark, twisted and terrifying.

"You don't wanna toss around some threats?" Aden snorts as he lays on the bed, massaging my feet.

"I don't need to. When we find the one responsible, I'm going to saw his useless little dick from his body and force him to eat it while his loved ones watch." Alec yawns over the phone and I don't think my eyes could widen any further. Aden's snicker has me ready to climb the walls.

"How can you be so calm?" I ask him. Alec speaks up, "Have you seen anyone stand against us and live to see another miserable day?"

CHAPTER TWENTY-SIX

Aden

Markus kept putting his damn froggy rain boots on my table and I was moments away from stabbing him with a fork for it. Nina comes back downstairs with Isabelle on her heels and Amelia skipping proudly ahead of them. She stops, frowning and she rests her tiny fists on her hips and glares at her father.

"Shoes on the table are bad." She huffs out at him and Markus drops his feet, looking ashamed as I smother a laugh. Amelia runs up to Gabby, the two form an immediate friendship and rush off to cause trouble in another room.

"Those two are going to be fierce when they're older." Isabelle shakes her head, letting Markus pull her into his lap. "When they're older? I saw the look in Amelia's eye, they're plotting something." Percy tsks, his smile dropping when he catches sight of Olivia. She's leaned close to Grayson, the two of them talking as they watch something on his phone.

Alec crosses his arms, looking Grayson over with a slow scowl. Under scrutiny, he stands taller, and drops his head in respect. Markus snorts, "You'll fit in if you drop the bow. Aden might act like a princess but you don't have to curtsy to us." Grayson chuckles, enjoying me being the butt of a joke.

My phone beeps, saving Alec. It's the front gate and my guard is waving frantically at the camera. I see my sister leaning over Jared in the front seat to chew the poor guy's head off.

"Let them through before she hurts you." I warn him, watching with amusement as she flips the camera off, their car speeding down the driveway.

"Nina, you and the ladies take the kids to the other room." I cross my arms, leaning my hip against the counter and Markus sucks a breath through his teeth, dragging his thumb across his throat to signal that I'm screwed.

"Because what, us women aren't useful in your big man plans?" Isabelle snarks, her fists perched on her hips exactly as Amelia had before. I see where she gets her attitude from.

"We are going to be helping in other ways," Nina steps forward, looking to me for support and I nod for her to keep going. "Olivia and Isabelle, you're going to help me get into their cameras, and we're going to screw up their weapon shipments that they've got coming. Then we can hack into their cameras, it'll give them the upper hand. It's going to take a while." She says, motioning them to follow her. Alec grips Isabelle, muttering in her ear as Markus slaps her ass. Their very open displays of affection are normal for most of us, but even Grayson looks uncomfortable and Olivia's face is bright red.

Percy has a look of longing in his eyes as he watches their interaction, his gaze cutting to Olivia before he rubs a hand across his forehead, as if he can scrub away the exhaustion. He and Grayson's attraction to the same woman is obvious. The both of them seeing two men, brothers at that, happily sharing the same woman could do one of two things. Inspire or create a rivalry. If I were a betting man, I'd say it's the latter of the two.

Jared walks in with his arm around Luna, keeping his body slightly in front of hers as he immediately assesses the two new men sitting in my kitchen.

"Why do you weirdos always have your little business tug circles in the dining room, yet you never set any snacks out?" Luna grumbles, limping past me as she heads towards the cabinets.

"Make yourself at home," I wave a hand. "Suck my dick." Luna says, walking past me with a bag of doritos. The bag Jared asked me to make sure we had on hand, because her cravings were do or die. She happily carries her snack hoard to the table, struggling against the jar of pickles before Jared pops them open, opening her cheese sticks as well.

"Say a fucking word, I dare you." She points her fork at each of us, juice dripping from the half of a pickle left as she chomps onto her cheese stick.

"You're an abomination," Markus has a horrified look on his face as he stares at her in mock fear. Jared's head snaps in his direction, and I ready myself to break up a fight.

"She's just biting chunks off of it, not even peeling it." Percy covers his mouth as he watches.

"It's string cheese, Luna. Can't you at least try to act civilized?" Alec shakes his head, amusement in his eyes. Jared coughs to cover his laugh as she takes another massive bite, drinking her pickle juice and munching on a chip. Nina had some wild cravings too, so I can't say I'm fazed. Grayson has been slowly stepping back, until he's against the wall and effectively out of our bubble. I remember the way Nina looked at me, with pride and love for me showing the man some mercy.

"If you run, I'll shoot you in the ankle." I warn him and he grins, shaking his head as some tension bleeds away. I clap my hands, getting everyone's attention as I step closer.

"We have a plan." I say, glancing at Alec. He nods once, coming to stand next to me as we fill everyone in on the hazardous, but potentially effective, plan.

Luna and Jared are chest to chest, and I can't decide who I should be backing at this point. Jared looks at me, and I can see the fear he hides so well as it claws its way to the surface. My sister is going to be pissed.

"Luna, you will stay here and help protect the kids. End of discussion." I say. Alec agrees, which sends her over the edge as the rest of us begin packing our weapons into the waiting cars.

"I'm meant to be on the field, and you swore that you'd treat me like an equal." She throws her hands up.

"I sure as fuck did. But I didn't make that deal with them," I point to her stomach and she crosses her arms, only getting more angry.

"You can handle yourself Lunatic, and nobody is trying to say otherwise, but you're not back to one hundred percent. Our daughter needs you to have just an ounce of self preservation, dammit." Jared huffs, checking his gun before pressing it into her hands as he leans to push his forehead against hers. "I can't lose you or her."

"A girl, huh? That's exciting, bud. Welcome to the happiest and scariest time of your life. *Fatherhood*." Markus grins, whistling to himself as he comes outside with the women on his tail. Luna gives a small smile, her hand dropping to cover Jared's as he rubs her lower stomach. Nina bumps her hip against mine, Leo immediately reaches his hand out to grab for me.

"I'll be with you the entire time, Aden." She promises. I hate seeing her so afraid, concerned for my safety more than her own.

"You're always with me, Nina."

"Come back to us in one piece." She demands more than pleads as my hand brushes her hair away from her face. "I will always come back to you, Nina. You are my home." I kiss her forehead, then Leo's before I turn to leave.

"If any of you die, I'll spit on your damn corpse." Luna warns us all, tucking Jared's gun into her waistband. The bravado is an act, and I can see the way she bites her lip as we climb into the cars.

"I'll name this baby after one of my exes if you die." Isabelle calls out, grinning like a fool as Alec rolls down the window and gives her a murderous glare. "You'll pay for that comment later, Darling." He grits out. She blows a kiss, winking at the brothers who share the same look of rage. Olivia is silent, watching with fear as Percy refuses to meet her eyes when climbing into another vehicle. Grayson looks pissed that I made him stay behind as well, but if things go to shit, I want somebody I trust here to get them somewhere safe.

CHAPTER
TWENTY-SEVEN

Nina

My fingers fly across the keyboard as Isabelle leans close to watch my movement. It used to bother and make me nervous when people gawked over my shoulder, but not anymore. Aden always reminds me that I should be proud of my hard work and knack for this. Luna's sitting on the floor watching Leo on his playmat, handing him his pacifier everytime he pops it from his mouth and throws it.

The screen flashes as windows start popping up over my screen, and Isabelle pumps her fist in the air. "You're a cyber genius, girl." She says excitedly. Luna scrambles to come next to us, pushing her head between mine and Olivia's as she watches intensely. David's team hacked into our security system the moment we lowered our defenses, just like we knew they would. The fact that they didn't appear to even question it is concerning.

But it also made way for me to break into their security system, disable their home alarm and play a looping feed on the security cameras that I had prepared this morning. It wasn't a permanent solution, but it would be enough for the men to get in before the entire mansion was on alert.

Leo starts fussing and Grayson brings him to me, turning his back as I quickly latch him on and keep going.

"You're a dang icon, Nina." Luna grins next to me and I preen a little under the complement. Isabelle taps the headphone in her ear, asking on repeat if anyone can hear her. We all wait, intensely staring at the phone that sits on the counter with the speaker on.

"We're pulling up now, are you ready?" Jared asks.

"There's four at the gate, and at least six more in the living room. The place has been turned into a camp for their entire army. Maybe we should just blow it up and call it quits." I mumble the last words and Jared chuckles.

"We would have to be extremely sneaky to pull it off, and even then, we don't have the explosives to blow this entire mansion to bits. We're going in old school, kid." He says. I hate when he calls me that and Luna rolls her eyes.

"Be nice, Biggums. Have fun for both of us." She says, absentmindedly rubbing a hand over her stomach.

"Camera's are down. Security system is disabled, you guys are as good to go as you can be." I sit back, my eyes flicking over the three monitors that are on the counter in front of me.

Something in my gut is screaming, warning me that this is wrong. But I tamper it down and keep my eyes on the screens. The sounds of gunshots popping off, followed by shouting and the sound of men dying has everyone holding their breath. Markus's laughter follows the moment of silence, and they keep with the plans on splitting up to take on three exits. They each take their places, and my access to the live video blacks out.

"Hold on, I just lost the cameras. Pull back until I can get them back up." Sweat covers my brow as I sit forward, desperately trying to figure out what went wrong.

Words flash across the screen, at the same moment each group bursts through the doors. "I told you to wait!" I shout, but their mics all crackle, the speaker emitting a high screech and disconnects.

"*Your life for his, knock knock.*" Isabelle reads, bracing one hand on the counter as she covers her mouth with the other. Grayson tilts his head, pulling his gun from its holster on his hip.

"Do you have a safe room here, a door that you can barricade, anything?" Grayson asks. I bite my lip, but nod once. "Don't try to be a hero Nina, take everyone there now." He puts his hand on my lower back, pushing me towards the stairs. He sits on his heel, taking his daughter's hand in his as he smiles.

"You are going to go with your new friend, and you'll stay right with Olivia. Do you understand?" Graysons tone is gentle and calm, but she throws her arms around his neck as he holds her tightly. When Olivia gently pulls her away Grayson nods to me once and turns towards the front door.

I rush everyone to the room, helping them through the door in my closet. But Luna refuses, trying to shove me in after Isabelle. I quickly pass Leo to Isabelle, and ignore her as she begins shouting at me. Luna and I slam the door shut and the lock clicks into place.

"You should have gone with them, this is stupid and dangerous." She chastices me. I give her a look, waving my hand up and down as she rolls her eyes and pulls out a gun.

"I actually have a weapon." She smirks. I drop under the bed, digging around until I pull out both hand guns and their clips from the case Aden keeps stashed. I can hear them now, people shouting outside and gunshots that make my jaw ache from how tightly I tense up. Luna just looks irritated as she creeps to the door, leaning against the frame while listening.

I pull out my cellphone to access our camera's and show her Gray standing bravely by the bottom steps, giving directions to the guards that stayed behind. He taps on his phone, pacing before throwing his hands up in agitation and pocketing it. My guess is that he called for help and nobody answered, But he doesn't waver.

I can't just let him die. Especially when the people breaking in were coming from the kitchen and would sneak up on him. I shove the phone into Luna's hands, popping an ear piece in as I run for the door.

"Where are you going?" She hisses, trying to follow.

"I need you here to give us back up. I'm going to get an earpiece for Grayson so we can all communicate and we are going to survive this." I tell her, shutting the door before she can argue. I don't miss the names she calls me, each one more colorful than the last while I roll my eyes and hurry down the hallway.

"Gray?" I keep my voice low, but the sound of glass breaking has my feet pounding over the floors. I lurch to a stop when I catch sight of him. Grayson's cheek is bleeding and he's rolling across the ground with a man who easily has thirty pounds on him. I raise the gun but can't take a shot without possibly hitting Grayson, and his eyes flick to mine.

"Behind, Nina!" He roars, launching the both of them sideways and I duck, spinning on my heel. A woman looks me over and I can see the hesitation as she lowers her gun just a fraction.

"They want me alive." The words slip out on a breath when I realize it. She steps closer and my finger tenses, pulling the trigger and lurching the gun in my hands. She drops her weapon, clutching her chest as blood pours from her wound and her body falls to the floor.

When I turn back to Grayson, he is on top of the other man, crushing his windpipe beneath his hands as he chokes the life from him. He looks like the grim reaper, with a skull tattooed on the back of his head and the curl of his lips.

"Gray, he's dead. You need to get up before more people come." I step closer, but he doesn't stop. My hand taps his shoulder and his head wrenches to turn an empty glare on me. "Gray, it's me." I say.

He visibly shakes himself, rubbing a hand across his face as he blinks rapidly.

"Obviously it's you," He grumbles, climbing off the man's body and grabbing his foot to drag him away. That's when I see the small pile of bodies, and my hands start shaking. Nausea is rolling through me and I press the back of my hand to my mouth to fight the bile as it threatens to spill.

"Nina, they were going to kill all of your friends. Even worse, it looks like they're under orders to bring you in alive. You don't have to enjoy killing, but don't fall apart over surviving." Grayson grips my shoulders, shaking me softly until I blow out a breath and nod once, following him past the woman I shot. He puts himself between me and her corpse, blocking my view as he grabs her gun.

"That hulk back there tossed my favorite fucking gun." He mutters, frowning as he swipes the blood off on his pant leg and keeps walking.

"*Sonofabitch,*" Luna roars as we stop at the back doors. The doors are wide open and she's laying in a bush, struggling to climb out as we both stare from the doorway. She sees us, flipping her middle finger up.

"Gonna watch the pregnant woman struggle or does somebody want to help before I get free and kick all your ankles in?" Luna is irritated, but I don't miss the amount of people lying across the backyard while Grayson easily helps her out.

"Nine, if you're counting. I definitely beat Biggums this time." She grins, doing a little dance as we walk towards the shed.

"Biggums?" Grayson raises his brow.

"Jared and Luna compete to see how many kills they can get any-time they're out on jobs and that's her nickname for him." I explain.

"Not because of how tall he is, it's because he has a massive," I bump into Luna as her words cut off. She throws her arm behind her, clutching my wrist as she pushes us back a step.

Looking like something dragged from beyond the grave, David lurches from the shed as he leans against two men, his snarl trained on me as they shuffle to a stop twenty feet away.

"Your husband is dead, Nina. There's nobody left to fucking save you now." He croaks, the gun in his hand dangerously bouncing as he shakes.

CHAPTER
TWENTY-EIGHT

Aden

This isn't going at all how we expected and each bullet that pierces the wall above my head sends another strike of irritation through me. They weren't just prepared for any simple attack, they were waiting for us specifically. Jared is still trying to wipe blood from his hand from crushing a man's skull. His eyes cut to me and he frowns.

"Didn't realize you could get any uglier. Luna really got all the looks." He taunts me but the worry sets into the corner of his eyes as his frown deepens. My head is still bleeding from a run in with a woman swinging a fire extinguisher. The gun shots finally taper off, and an older man screams for everyone to take cover.

Markus dives across us, covering his head as he hides behind the flipped desk we are using just as a massive explosion rocks the building. Debris and dust rain around us and my ears start to ring. My vision is clouded and I cough to clear my lungs. Markus pops his head up, wagging his dark eyebrows at me with a cheshires smirk on his face.

"Alec needs us, let's get a move on ladies." He peers between us, content that he's taken care of the group that had us pinned only moments ago. The scene has gone from tragic to gruesome, with a portion of the wall blown away and bodies littered among the rubble.

I don't have time to feel guilt or remorse for the people sent to kill us when I'm following Markus' heels as we race for the stairs. Taking them two at a time we stop at the landing.

"Fuck," Jared spits the word, and I can hear the way his teeth grind together as he looms over my shoulder. Alec is standing completely still, his arms crossed and a brow quirked as if he's just bored.

The tick in his jaw followed by the way his eyes flicker across each of us, assessing for injuries, is a dead giveaway. He's pissed and moments away from losing his false calm demeanor. A gun is pressed to his temple, and he rolls his eyes as if it's just another nuisance.

"David's loose. They've got the women. Go." He demands. I can feel myself being pulled towards home, to where everyone we treasure is waiting for us to come save them.

"You've got a big mouth, ya know that? Run to save her, and he fucking dies." The heavy set man holding Alec's life in his hands smirks, his thick blonde beard bouncing as he smacks his gum.

They're both drenched in sweat, their clothes torn in places and covered in dust. The multiple dead bodies and blood soaked gun laying around the room shows how much of a fight Alec put up. Percy is watching every move, his gun raised and ready in one hand, but his other arm is held close to his chest and I can see the blood soaking his shirt.

"I run for backup and you have all the fun." Markus has gone deathly still next to me, his words cold and guttural. His lip is curled back in a snarl, and the shine in his eyes is beyond feral. Jared shifts behind me, making room for me to pass. I can feel his unease, a duty to both families. One that I'm familiar with, since I've begun to see these men as my brothers.

"Lower your gun. This doesn't have to end with more death." I keep my voice low, ducking my head to give a more docile appearance. Markus cuts his gaze to mine, shock and something else swirl across his face before his eyes are once again on the man threatening his brother's life. Alec gives me a look that could kill, and I return it with a smile.

"Boy, none of us is living to see tomorrow. Mrs. K won't rest 'till you're all good and dead." The man says, cracking his neck and pushing the barrel harder to Alec's head. I hold my hands up, trying to keep his focus on me. Jared, Markus or Percy will get an opening to take their shot eventually. I just have to make sure he doesn't splatter Alec's brain across the wall before then. Isabelle won't survive losing either of her husbands.

"If she kills us then she'll never see David alive again." But it's not fully true, David is still alive. The man laughs, shaking his head at us.

"Do you really believe that's the only reason she's after you? You boys have been incurring her wrath for many years now. Especially you, big guy." He tips his head towards Jared. Alec's head jerks up, as if the answer is written on the hideous red wallpaper above our heads.

"Stefan," He mutters, and I nearly whip around to see what he's staring at. Alec wrenches forward, knocking the gun from the man's grip and sending it clattering to the ground. Markus puts the man down immediately, his body flinging backwards the moment the bullet strikes his forehead.

"What the fuck was he on about?" Markus rushes forward, grabbing his brother in a tight hug. Alec cups the back of his head, ruffling his messy hair as he smirks.

"Who is Stefan? David mentioned him before." Percy winces, doing his best to hide the discomfort from the wound in his arm.

"When their father, James Barone, hired me, I was given my first big job. I was sent to burn a house down that was allegedly full of stolen weapons." Jared looks ill, his face paler as he struggles to find the right words. "There was a woman and her daughter inside, but by the time I realized it, I couldn't get them out."

"She was our fathers mistress, and was pregnant with his child. That woman was Stefan's mom. The reason he kept coming after us, after our territory and family, was more than just rivalry. Our father is continuing to make life hell for us from the damn grave." Markus grumbles, picking a cigarette out from the crushed pack in his pocket.

"That still doesn't explain what David's mother has to do with this." Irritation laces my voice and Alec walks towards the stairs. "David Killinger was Stefan's cousin. Their mothers were sisters."

The painting is slightly crooked, the image of a petite blonde woman. Her smile doesn't quite reach her eyes as she leans against a larger woman. They share the same features, same hair color and I can see the resemblance David once shared with them. Before I mutilated his face. Jared turns away from the image with a hand on his chest. I grip his shoulder, forcing his eyes to meet mine.

"You were the right hand to a cruel and twisted man. He manipulated you into burning down a building that you thought was empty. If you had questioned him or his orders, you would have been killed and another poor bastard would have been sent to finish the job." I remind him. Jared nods once, but the guilt doesn't ease.

"It's silent." Markus points out.

"I think we either killed everyone, they evacuated, or they're after the women." Alec points out.

"Or the place is boobie trapped." Markus points to a cluster of brightly colored wires peeking out from under a dirty cloth.

We all rush for the stairs.

A second too late.

The explosion rocks the entire house, sending each of us hurtling in different directions as the building crumbles around us.

CHAPTER TWENTY-NINE

Nina

My heart thunders behind my ribs, drowning out all other sounds until I shake my head. He has to be wrong, Aden can't be dead. My throat is dry, and I struggle to swallow back the bile as it rises from my stomach. Luna inches closer, trying to put herself in front of me protectively.

"You're a liar. You wouldn't let anyone else have the satisfaction of killing him." She tries to sound confident, but her voice still wobbles. David smiles, and the sight makes me want to vomit. His entire body is covered in bruises, from yellow to deep blue and his eyes are sunken in. Dried blood crusts his face and arms, one of his hands is swathed in a thick bandage and he struggles to blink.

"He was an idiot for letting me live, I won't make the same mistake. I wanted him to watch me break the wife he stole from me, but that isn't a risk I'm willing to take." David points his gun at Grayson, and I shove myself between them.

"Nina, step back." Grayson snaps. But I keep my chin up and shake my head once.

"Leo needs you. If what he says is true, that boy needs you." His voice is low, meant only for me to hear. My stance wavers, and Grayson shoves me behind him.

"What a hero," The woman under David's right arm smirks, and my heart aches when I recognize her.

"Anne," disbelief makes me want to deny what I'm seeing but there's no reasonable explanation. For just a moment, she looks at me with guilt but immediately covers it by rolling her eyes.

"Don't be pathetic. In war, you have to pick a side." My previous bodyguard dismisses me. David grins and the feeling of helplessness grows. What if Aden is dead? Grayson and Luna didn't have a chance of taking on the half dozen other men that step up behind David and his two lackeys.

"You are hurt, sweet boy." A woman's high pitched voice calls, and I turn to see the woman who trapped me in our marriage arrangement all those years ago.

Hannah Killinger, David's mother. The disgust on her face as she passes me is the same as it was the day we met and she declared I was a poor choice for her son. The cold metal that digs into my jaw can't be mistaken for anything else. A hand threads through my hair, fisting tight to wrench me back against a hard chest. The smell of cheap cologne and cigarettes makes me want to turn away, but I keep my body still. Before Grayson can turn, two men flank him and Luna is grabbed by another.

"Awful lot of effort for something so plain," The man behind me chuckles, his warm breath fanning my neck. Hannah stands near David, not reaching out to him as she frowns at his appearance. He stands taller, always the boy who wants his mothers approval. Disgust replaces the pity I fleetingly felt for him.

"Had a bit of a pest issue, but the problem has been dealt with. I do believe it's time to finish this. Bring that one to me," Hannah's eyes light up with malice, their intensity growing as Luna is wrenched by her arm towards the woman. She fights the entire way, thrashing and clawing until the man jams the barrel of his gun into her ribs.

"Would you prefer to bleed out in the dirt or cooperate?" Hannah waves her hand, and I try to jerk forward, desperate to do anything to protect Luna. The man holding me grunts, but doesn't budge.

"Move and I'll kill the traitor and his bastard child." Hannah pulls a gun from the pocket of her pantsuit, pointing it at Grayson as he struggles against the two men holding him.

"Touch my daughter and I'll kill you." Grayson snarls. They kick the backs of his knees, forcing him to kneel as his arms are wrenched painfully behind his back. This can't be happening. If Hannah is here, that means Aden is dead or trapped. My heart starts thundering as Hannah leans close to Luna, gripping her face harder until I can see her fingers digging into her cheeks.

"Let her go, this is my fault. She's innocent." I plead, trying to reason with Hannah. But her frigid glare stops me, and it's plain to see she's beyond conversation.

"Innocent? Her barbaric husband took somebody I love from me, not once, but twice. And her brother sealed your fate when he dared to steal my sons betrothed. Our family has been torn down many times over and it will stop here and now." Hannah steps back, straightening her clothes as she looks towards me with hatred.

"Jared accepted a job to burn down a building, he didn't know that woman was inside." Luna is fiercely protective of him, and she holds her chin high as she defends him.

"That *woman* was my sister, and she was knocked up with an heir of the Barone family. She was a coward and tried to run from her destiny, from the power we could have had. As if that wasn't enough, you all had a hand in killing my nephew Stefan when he took you in! He could have been something great. You ungrateful whores were all offered a chance to support powerful men and chose *this*." She spits the words.

"Stefan kidnapped Amelia to use her as leverage for the Barone's territory. He deserved to die." Luna spits on Hannah's shoes and panic grips me as the woman raises her hand, the sound of skin striking skin cracks across the quiet yard. Luna's face whips to the side from the slap, and blood wells from the corner of her lip.

"Stop, you don't have to do this!" I plead, but Hannah is beyond listening.

My mind races as I devour what she says. I want to feel sympathy for her, but the ache in my chest as I think of Aden holds me back. David is a monster, born from a power hungry family and it was easy to see where he got it from. But I can't give up. Aden would want me to fight.

"Where are they hiding?" Hannah asks. I shake my head once, refusing to betray them. She shrugs, flicking her hand and sending two of her people towards my home. I don't waver, knowing that they won't find them.

"Burn the building with them all in it." Her words carve through my chest and fear floods my veins. "Then kill these three as they listen to the screams and know every death was at their hands." She smiles, clapping her hands excitedly.

CHAPTER THIRTY

Aden

I'm dead. Or dying. Maybe I'm just really, really concussed? My muscles won't cooperate, only moving to lurch me onto my side as a coughing fit violently racks my entire body. The taste of copper follows the wet splatter in my mouth and I swipe it away with my sleeve, or what's left of my now tattered clothing. The damn high pitched ringing was going to drive me to insanity before anything else.

I force my eyes to blink, slowly flinching against the bright blur that waits for me. Memories flood back as I clutch my head and finally sit up. The explosion, David is free and Nina is in danger. I have to get up and find everyone else but when I pull my hand away from my head, it's covered in a sticky layer of blood and grime. My vision finally clears and I'm sitting in the rubble of what's left of the house.

Portions of the walls are still standing, and a few stairs are digging into my back where I lean against them. Random bits of furniture and other debris cover my body as I slowly pull myself free. Everything hurts, but Nina needs me. She needs me to push through.

"You look like shit," A familiar voice wheezes, and Jared shakes his head, sending bits of dust and drywall fluttering around us.

"Wait until you find a mirror and realize that you are actually looking better with a black eye and a powdered face. Hides the gray hair." I smirk as he flips his middle finger towards me.

"Bunch of cockroaches, you're all unkillable." Markus smiles, a cigarette dangling from his lip and he leans against a portion of wall. Alec is sitting next to him, glaring at his brother. "I saved him and he's pissed off about it." Markus points his thumb at Alec as he gets to his feet, dusting his hands off.

"If you pull me by the hair again, I'll break every bone in your hand." Alec mutters, pushing past him and leading all of us outside. Percy wheezes out a cough as he shakes his head, sending debris flying from his dusty blue hair.

"Ungrateful," Markus mumbles. "You like it when Isabelle pulls your hair."

Alec doesn't dignify that with a response as we all stagger around the crumbling home and dead bodies. The more my strength returns, the more impatient I become to get home. We have a safe room that is damn near impenetrable, but my mind keeps running through the 'what ifs'. What if they didn't make it inside, or if they are lured out?

The entire drive back is silent, tension palpable as we gather the few surviving men. We were all worse off than I'd like, but we can lick our wounds when this is over. We will finish it tonight. I was at the center of Hannah's rage.

My best friend had married the two men that inherited the Barone legacy. My sister's husband had killed Hannah's sister and nephew. Then I had swooped in to steal away David's bride to be, tried to kill him, and then left him for dead in our shed all these years later. I finally catch sight of my house, but it's not my home. Flames flick along the wall, crawling higher as I tear my seatbelt off and race from the car before we even make it to the gate. The doors are thrown wide open and useless, as if the fire isn't enough warning that we might be too late.

"They won't survive long in the safe room, if they're even in it" I shout, not checking to see if I'm charging headfirst into this alone.

"Let me go!" Nina's shrill scream has me turning to race for the backyard, but Jared grabs my collar and yanks me to a stop before I can round the side of the house.

"Be fucking smart. They'll drop you the moment they see you." He mutters through clenched teeth.

"We don't have time, that's why I texted you for backup earlier." Alec huffs into his phone, all calm has bled from his features. "I was a little busy with a gun to my head. Your daughter and granddaughter are in danger, if I'm asking you for help then it's obviously serious." Alec hangs up and pockets his phone.

"We need to make this quick, Lucian is sending his men but if anyone is inside," Alec trails off, and we don't need to be told twice. Alec and Jared head into the front of the house, taking the one measly fire extinguisher we have in the garage. As if things can't get worse, we inch through the massive garage and I peer through the back window, staying low to the ground. The sight makes me want to rush out and snap David's neck like I should have done days ago. Markus grips the window frame as he leans closer, and I know he's skimming the faces for her.

"My girls are in that fucking inferno." His composure crumbles, and I know that we are running out of time. Percy is struggling to stay upright, and I help him lean against the wall and slide to the ground. "You've lost a lot of blood, but you'll be alright, kid." I pat his face and he gives a ghost of a smile.

"Take the first opening you see." I tell Markus, opening the door and strolling out with a forced look of boredom on my face.

"You have to be kidding me. He just wont fucking die." David tries to shout, but it comes out more like a strangled whimper. Probably from the multiple lacerations on his tongue, poor pitiful guy.

"I could say the same for you, buddy. You're looking different, one of those trendy diets and some plastic surgery? It suits you." I shrug with a smirk, keeping my eyes trained forward as Nina lunges against the man restraining her. First David was going to die, but the man with his hands on my wife is next.

Anne is helping shoulder David's weight, and she avoids looking at me with shame written across her face. I won't give second chances to people like her. Luna leans sideways to peer past me, her eyes widening. She bites down onto the man's arm that holds her, making him fire a shot that narrowly misses her head. The bullet hits the other man that was holding David up, and they begin to fall over. Hannah waves her hand, but before she can demand one of her lackeys do anything, a glass bottle sails overhead.

I recognize the fuzzy green sock sticking out the top, that inevitably has a frog on the side. *Markus.* He was alone for less than ten minutes and he made an explosive from random junk in my garage and his stupid sock.

I launch myself sideways, slamming Nina and the man behind her to the ground while knocking the gun from his hand. The explosion bursts heat across my back, licking at my legs as we roll and I wrench her from his grasp. Her tear stained cheeks send a rush through me.

The small explosion only gives us a moment to react, and I jump to my feet, firing through the smoke and flames that crawl over the dead leaves. David's body flies backwards, being dragged down by Anne's limp body. Hannah is gone, vanished from sight along with a few of the idiots she brought with her. I swing sideways, shooting the man that was holding Nina back and I take a sick satisfaction from it. Grayson is helping Luna to her feet, and I nod to him once.

Markus is stomping across the yard, a cigarette hanging from his lip as he walks barefoot towards me. Percy is standing tall, holding his gun up as he whips his head around to watch the entire yard. I help Nina up, holding her tight to my side as wipes her dirty face with the back of her hand. She kisses my cheek, then turns and tries to run towards the house. I wrap an arm around her waist and tear her feet from the ground to slam her back against my chest.

"Our son is in there!" She cries, fighting against my hold.

"That's why I need to know you'll stay here, where it is safe. I have to focus on getting him out of there and I can't do that if I'm worried about you. Understood?" I snap, shoving her towards Markus as I turn and race towards the house.

Out of the frying pan.

CHAPTER THIRTY-ONE

Aden

I should be dripping sweat, but the heat is evaporating every droplet as it forms on my skin. I helped build this house, and knew it better than anyone else so it doesn't take me long to rush through the growing smoke cloud. Thankfully the flames were at the front of the building, but they will rip through the rest of the house within minutes. My shoes slide across the blood puddles that cover the bright stone floors, but I don't stop as I round the stairs and take them two at a time.

"Maybe next time we should ask where the damn safe room is first," Jared's voice catches my attention from Leo's room as they throw furniture around, searching for the hidden door.

"Closet, my room!" I shout, not stopping for anything as I rush into the bedroom. The closet door snaps partially off of its hinges from the force I use to throw my body against it. I stop in front of the control panel set into the wall.

The panel is sparking, a bullet hole in the center and I glare back at the dead body on my floor. Somebody tried to break in. Panic sets in as I stare, my entire body motionless as I think through my options. Finally I reach out and rip the box from the wall, exposing the wiring behind it and snap the back of my phone off.

"There's a fire extinguisher in Leo's room, in his closet. Buy me some time." I shout, not looking back as I begin working to rewire it directly to my phone. It's not a guaranteed fix, but it's better than hoping for a miracle. My chest burns, stinging as I cough to clear my lungs just for them to be tighter on each breath. I hear them using the fire extinguisher, but I know it's a bandaid over a bullet hole. This fire isn't going to stop until it has devoured everything in its path, which includes us.

It feels like an eternity later when the screen lights up for me to input a code to release the doors. Jared has soaked blankets in water from the bathroom in the few minutes it has taken me to break inside of the safe room and he hands them to each of us. I quickly drop the mangled phone and leap to my feet, watching as the door pops free. A shoe flies past and narrowly misses my head.

"I'll gut you if you step near us, you giant pussies!" Isabelle's voice wavers, giving away the hint of fear.

"You're safe, darling. It's us." Alec rushes forward and she steps out of the shadows with wide eyes. "You're here? You are all here and you're okay?" Her lip quivers as he gathers her close.

"Luna is outside, she's safe." I tell Jared when I see the disappointed look on his face. He nods once, taking Gabby from Olivia's arms. "My sister?" She asks, glancing back at the cameras as they flicker in and out on the desk in the safe room.

"She's okay, we need to get you all out of here." I say as Isabelle hands Leo to me. Alec scoops up Amelia and we keep our bodies hunched low as we rush through the house as it fills with smoke. The blankets help protect the children against some of the heat and smoke, but we don't have much time.

That's when a siren breaks through the inferno, making me tilt my head as I listen. Firetruck meant cops weren't far behind them, we needed to finish this before they put a stop to the madness. I couldn't let David walk away from this, he would face justice for his crimes by my hand only. As we stop next to the stairs and I crouch low as the smoke becomes thicker.

"Form a chain, Olivia you grab onto me and Jared. Isabelle you grab Jared and Alec, nobody lets go and don't stop!" I shout, trying to stay calm over the sound of the children's quiet cries.

The front of the house is nearly engulfed in fire as we race for the door, breaking through and not slowing down until everyone is scattered on the lawn. Leo is inconsolable as I rock him, just grateful that he's alive. Gabby is clinging to Jared silently as he rocks her, and Amelia sobs loudly into Alec's neck.

Isabelle and Olivia are both pale, and I'm grateful for the firetruck that races over my driveway, flanked by an ambulance. I kiss my son, laying him in Olivia's arms before I run around the side of the house. We are so close, and the Barone's influence over the cops can only go so far.

Nina is staring down at the ground where she kneels with blood soaking the front of her shirt and Grayson is leaning against Percy. They both look at me with concern and my heart threatens to burst from my chest. The closer I get, the harder my pulse thrums in my ears, drowning out all sound.

Nina is soaked in blood, but it isn't hers. David is dead. His jaw is slack, eyes glazed over as he lays motionless with scratch marks marking his neck. I reach out, gently grabbing Nina by the shoulder and she drags her eyes to meet mine.

"Are you hurt?" I ask. She frowns, her brows drawing together as if the possibility hadn't crossed her mind. Nina slowly shakes her head, looking down at her bloody hands. I notice the nails are ripped and bent, and pull her to her feet as I look to Grayson and Percy for answers.

"He attacked her. Prick shot me in the leg when I tried to stop him, and Percy was chasing down this coward's mother." Grayson spits on David's corpse, and I gain a little more appreciation for him. "I shot him when he dropped his gun trying to choke her."

"He's dead. Really dead." Nina's voice is broken and soft enough that I nearly miss her words. I kiss the top of her head, holding her tighter. "He's gone, my heart. For good this time, but we have one more loose end to tie up."

Markus is whistling as he walks, and Luna has a grin on her face that makes me want to back away as they come closer. Through the smoke and embers on the ground, Markus is dragging something attached to a rope. "Don't say I never got you anything." Markus winks.

She screams when her back is dragged across the ground that still crawls with flames and charred bits of kindling. Hannah's arms and hands are bound. I don't feel like a monster from the excitement that courses through me. Luna holds out her hand, a massive knife resting in her palm as she gives me the honors. I shift Nina to her arms, nodding to my sister as I step over to smile down at Hannah.

"Be glad I don't have time to play," I smile as she cries, shaking her head and fighting against the fabric that gags her. "Crossing my family was the biggest mistake you made, second to raising that pathetic sack of shit." I motion towards David with the knife, watching as her eyes widen before I plunge the knife into her chest.

I pull the knife free and offer it back to Luna, but she curls her lip in disgust. "I don't want that bitches blood on me, she was extra mean." She huffs and I drop the blade. Nina throws herself into my arms and I pick her up, holding her tight as I walk back to the front of the house where our families are waiting.

CHAPTER THIRTY-TWO

Nina

The next few hours seem to flow in a blur as I hold my son close, watching every paramedic as they check us over. Aden won't take more than a step away, his hand always touching me as he answers questions, and finally ushers me into the backseat of our car. Aden letting go of my hand is what finally brings me from my haze as I blink, realizing we were sitting in front of Luna and Jared's house. They were both turned from the front seat, staring at me as if waiting for me to say something.

"Jared offered to get Leo settled, if you and Aden would like to shower." Luna says gently. My door swings open and Aden unbuckles my seat belt, helping me to stand.

"I'm not breakable, Aden. Don't treat me like the word fragile is painted on my face." I reach into the car, careful not to wake our sleeping baby as I pick him up. "You may not be fragile, my love. But you are precious, and I will treat you how I fucking see fit. I've nearly lost you, the both of you, more times than I care to count." Aden snaps, putting his hand on my lower back to guide me towards the front door. My irritation fades as quickly as it came, leaving guilt in its wake.

Jared has his arm around Luna's shoulders and she leans heavily on him as we step inside. Their home is beautiful, hidden from the world by the trees that surround it. The interior is painted a dark shade of green, everything inside is dark and fitting of those who live here.

"Use our bathroom, there's a bathtub and a shower." Luna pushes us towards the stairs and Jared grunts his annoyance. Luna rolls her eyes, "We are sharing the guest bathroom shower, so stop pouting." she pokes his chest, and his angry demeanor melts away.

Aden fills the tub as I lean against the sink and stare at my reflection. Bruises mark the left side of my face, and my split lip that was starting to heal is swollen and covered in dried blood. Aden reaches around my body, using one hand to pull the hem of my shirt up and over my head while cradling Leo in his free arm.

"You need to shower, and this little guy could use a bath. The water is nice and warm." Aden unclasps my bra and slides it off gently, his fingers brushing along my skin. The intimacy of it all makes my heart flutter as he bends down to pull my pants off. Aden stands, his eyes locked on mine as he cradles my jaw in his hand, his fingers sliding around to burrow into my hair.

"Not today, but one day, this will be behind us. Nothing and no one will ever take you from me again, my heart." He presses his lips to my forehead, not caring for the sweat and layer of grime that covers us. I wrap my arms around his waist and allow myself to savor this moment, to feel the happiness I've been afraid of. Worried that if I let joy in, it would be ripped out from beneath me once again.

Aden guides me to the shower, holding my arm until I'm standing beneath the spray and letting it wash away the weight I'm carrying. Even if I know it will come back the moment we have to step back into the real world, but that's for another day. Today, I'll just be grateful we're all alive.

Aden closes the glass shower door and I slowly sink to the ground, letting the hot water wash over me as I listen to my husband sing to our son. The soft giggles and sounds of Leo's excited splashing is what sends me over the edge. I cover my mouth, burying my face in my knees as sobs wrack my body.

The water slowly turns colder, until the door opens and I peer up to see Aden lean in and adjust the temperature. A new cloud of steam starts to fill the space and I curl in tighter on myself as he steps inside and picks me up. "Leo is with his aunt and uncle being spoiled rotten, before you ask." He says. "Olivia is staying at Isabelle's house and she's safe. Percy and Grayson will be staying to work for the Barone's for the time being as well. I'm sure that will work out well." Sarcasm drips from his tone.

Aden sits with his back against the wall, and tucks my head under his chin while cradling me in his lap. My body relaxes as I press my face to his chest and soak in the heat coming off of him and the water. A small smile tugs at my lips, knowing that Aden hates hot showers but he would suffer through anything for me. I shift my body, turning to straddle him to get closer and Aden groans. When I try to sit up, he presses my head back to his chest and wraps his other arm around me.

"I want to take care of you and I'm trying to behave, my love. But you are fucking temptation itself." He swallows hard, and I laugh against his chest. He reaches up, stretching until he knocks down the different bottles of body wash and shampoo. He sighs, staring at the first bottle.

"I hate the smell of lavender." Aden mutters, glaring at the soap as if it has offended him. I relax as his large hands massage the shampoo into my scalp, the tender yet prodding sensation nearly puts me to sleep until he rinses it out and applies conditioner.

Aden helps me stand, opening the door to grab wash clothes from the counter. The rush of cold air makes me shiver, sucking in a breath and Aden stops with the soap bottle hovering above a washcloth as he stares at my chest before closing his eyes and sighing. The frigid air has my nipples hard and pointed, but Aden steps forward and starts washing my neck and shoulders.

I rest my hands on his sides, pulling us closer and stretching up to my tiptoes to kiss him. Which was a terrible idea in a slippery shower. I lose footing and fall against Aden, knocking him backwards against the wall as he catches us. He raises a brow, "Throwing yourself at me? I'm flattered." I roll my eyes, but don't move away from him. I don't want to leave our bubble until the water runs cold, which doesn't take all that long.

CHAPTER THIRTY-THREE

Aden

I should be exhausted, but sleeping in an unfamiliar house has me on edge and I am afraid I would wake Nina or Leo if I don't force myself downstairs. Jared is sitting on the couch in flannel pajama pants and a plain gray t-shirt, and I sigh as I sit down a short distance away from him.

"I gave you shirts, put your tits away." He mutters, but there's no venom in his tone.

"Leo was really worked up being in a strange place, he spit up while I was rocking him." I shrug. Jared chuckles at this, the darkness hides most of his features as we both sit in the silence until I speak up. "Uneasy with guests in your home?"

"Yes," Jared huffs, "But it's more than that. Luna has always been able to take care of herself, and she is a fucking force. But now, our daughter is growing inside of her and seeing her continue to be reckless is just," He shakes his head and stops speaking. I lean forward and rest my elbows on my knees as I stare down at my entwined fingers.

"It never gets any easier, I'm still pissed at Nina for handing herself over without saying a word to me. Then I find out she shoved everyone else into the safe room and ran off with Luna to protect them? Soon you won't be the only one with gray hair." Jared snorts, "Luna is smart, and like you said, she's a menace."

"A menace?" Luna says, crossing her arms as she stares daggers at Jared in the dark. I grin like a fool as I fold my hands behind my head and lean back. Until she steps into the room and the moon glow lights up her bare legs.

"Put some fucking pants on," I groan, grabbing a pillow and throwing it at her. She catches it and flips me her middle finger before throwing it back.

"A menace to my sanity, absolutely. I'm benching you. No more runs, no more jobs until this one is in college," Jared crosses the room, brushing his hand against her stomach as he towers over her. Luna scoffs, taking a step back and glaring at me past his arm.

"You big bad men come to this conclusion on your own? What makes you think you can just make this decision for me, is it because I'm a woman? You don't own me, Biggums." Luna crosses her arms, but Jared leans closer and her eyes widen.

"I own you, just as you own me. Maybe I should fucking remind you." Jared takes a step closer as she backs up.

"This is worse than watching my house burn to the ground." I groan, covering my face with a pillow as I slide sideways on the couch to lay down. Luna's squeal followed by her excited giggle as she races for the stairs is what puts me into motion. I pull my cell phone out and call Alec.

He answers on the second ring, "Anybody dying?" He asks.

"No, but why are you up at four in the morning?"

"I could ask you the same thing. What do you want? My wife isn't very patient and if I don't get this banana split back to her in the next five minutes, I won't get to eat it off her body when she changes her mind halfway through it." I can hear the smirk in his voice.

"You are all depraved perverts. I need a contractor, a good one that can be quick." I start pacing, excited at the idea of building our next home exactly how Nina would want. Her little comments about specific lighting, color schemes and everything else is at the front of my mind and I needed to get somebody started on this right away.

Jared and I were going to kill each other. Cramming the two of us in this house for four months was wearing everyone's patience down to slivers. Especially since jobs were slow, mostly moving weaponry and simple tasks that didn't let us expend any pent up energy. While Luna and Nina are upstairs cooing over the nursery as they insist on painting the walls a pale lavender, Jared and I are tasked with unloading the furniture from the truck.

"I was just saying that I'm not surprised you drive an oversized truck," I shrug, picking up the large box with the crib pieces inside. "I didn't even make the big truck, little dick joke."

Jared clamps his hand over it, slamming it back to the bed of the truck and blowing an irritated breath through his nose. He has decided to quit smoking before the baby gets here, and I was shockingly good at getting on his nerves.

"You lose speaking privileges, boy."

"I'm not-"

"Not another word." He cuts me off, yanking the crib away and stomping across the snow towards the front door. I can't help but smile as Nina stands on the porch with her arms crossed and an irritated look trained on me.

"Stop poking the bear, before he beats you. Or worse, Luna gets her hands on you." She warns me. Now that was a scary thought, Luna has become even more unhinged than before. I accidentally ate the last of her Doritos and she tried to strangle me with the bag.

"We should go out for lunch." I change the subject, walking up to her until we are eye to eye with her two stairs above me. She shrugs, running her fingers through my hair. "You don't want to help Jared put all the furniture together?" She teases.

"No," Jared shoots me a glare as he brushes past us to close the tailgate. I shrug, grabbing Nina by the back of her thighs to wrap her legs around my waist and walk her backwards into the house. Just as I lean in to kiss her, my phone rings from my back pocket and I want to throw it at a wall. Nina giggles, dropping her feet to the ground as she pats my chest.

"What?" I snap, not checking to see who it is.

"We have a new mission, pissy pants." Markus says, and I glance at Nina. She waves her hand towards the door.

"Have fun," She kisses me, but it's just a short peck and drives me wild. I don't waste any time rushing for my car, excited that I might be getting a real mission finally. I was an idiot.

I pull up to the front of Markus and Alec's house to a flurry of pink balloons and irritation that I can't keep off of my face. Markus is standing out front with too many boxes, each one is open and revealing the explosion of baby shower decorations.

"Is this my mission?" I snap, rolling my window down. Markus nods, and I weigh the possibility of running him over with my damn car. "It's for Luna, so get out here and put those pretty little lips to good use and blow these." He grins, holding out a handful of balloons. I still don't know how Isabelle hasn't stabbed him yet.

But I get out of the car, forcing myself to help with the decorations for her surprise baby shower.

Jared was going to hate it, which made me feel a little bit better.

Chapter Thirty-Four

Nina

Luna looks absolutely radiant in her puffy gray dress, with her bright hair braided away from her face. I smile with pride when I realize she has skipped foundation, leaving her scars on full display. They are a part of her, and another hint at the brave and beautiful woman I was currently watching scarf down canned cheese and banana peppers in the backseat of the car. She glares at me, "Why are you staring at me like that?"

"No judgment here, I ate vanilla ice cream with chopped jalapenos in it." I shrug and she gags, waving me away as we pull up to Isabelle's house.

"You better have a good reason for us wearing these fancy clothes," she reminds me, again. I roll my eyes and don't bother telling her to trust me for the hundredth time. She fights against the blindfold, but I worked too hard to keep her distracted for it to blow up now. When we finally come to a stop and I open the door, she doesn't expect Jared to take her hand in his.

"Biggums?" She breathes, confused. He helps her out of the car, steadying her on her feet as he guides her to the front door and inside. I press a hand to my lips, trying not to laugh at the adorable way she waddles. Jared pulls the blindfold away and smiles as she looks around in wonder. Isabelle, Olivia and I are all standing in front of a table piled high with gifts, and another table stacked with all of her pregnancy cravings. The men vanish quickly, leaving us to laugh, cry and enjoy being together in a way we haven't since everything happened with David.

I find myself extremely sentimental as I take my sister's hand in mine, squeezing tight while looking at my two best friends, both of them enjoying their pregnancy with a sense of serenity that I can feel myself sinking into.

By the time we are getting ready to leave, Luna is struggling to keep her eyes open and Isabelle is trying to rub her very swollen feet. Grayson offers to walk Olivia to her car, and I can see Percy clench his fists before he leaves the room. Isabelle catches me looking after him and waves me closer.

"I've been keeping an eye on the two of them. They're both hopelessly in love with your sister. Unfortunately I don't think it will work out for them quite the way it did for me." She leans back in the chair, sighing as Alec kneels at her feet and begins massaging them.

"You outdid yourself, my Darling. Let's get you to bed." He grins, helping her to her feet as Aden wraps his arm around my waist. Leo is snoring in the crook of Aden's arm, his tiny hand dangling off the side as we walk towards the car. The ride back to Jared and Luna's house sets into my body how tired I am, but I realize quickly that we are heading the wrong way.

Aden is smiling from the driver's seat and his hand grips my thigh tighter in anticipation.

"I don't suppose you wanna tell me where we are going?" I ask. He laughs, shaking his head. "The surprises aren't done quite yet." It isn't long before we pull into a long driveway, stopping at the gates, and he reaches through the window to punch in a code. The gates swing open and we drive along a paved driveway with freshly planted trees on each side.

The house we park in front of takes my breath away, the beautiful stone walls and Ivy that is placed along them look like something out of a fairytale. Aden gets out, carefully taking Leo from his seat before opening my door. I can't take my eyes off the beautiful home as we approach the dark wooden door, and he presses a piece of cold metal into my hand.

"Aden, I don't understand?" I ask, afraid to hope that this could be what I think it is. He shrugs, gently pushing my arm towards the door. I insert the key and twist, my heart racing as the lock slides open and I turn the handle. The entryway is dark, but the lights along the front of the driveway illuminate enough for me to step inside and fumble along the wall until a switch clicks beneath my shaking hand. I hold my breath as I look at the house I had dreamed of, with beautiful wood floors, vaulted ceilings and soft gray walls.

"Welcome home, my heart." Aden kisses the side of my head as he takes my hand in his, pulling me further inside. The living room is directly to our left, and a large black sectional takes up a portion of the large room. I smile at the sight of all the new toys Leo will no doubt spend tomorrow attached to. Aden doesn't give me time to gawk as he pulls me towards the kitchen to our right. The built-in breakfast nook, and the dark wooden cabinets set onto yellow walls makes me cover my mouth as I fight back tears.

"This is everything I have always dreamed of, Aden. How did you find it?" I ask.

"Alec put me in touch with an amazing contractor, I just told them every detail I could remember you mentioning." When I can't find the words to say what this means to me, I grab the sides of his face, pulling him closer to kiss him. He chuckles against my lips, and pulls away.

"There's more, come on." His boyish excitement makes my chest flutter as he pulls me to the stairs, and when we step up into the large landing I shake my head. The portraits on the walls are of us, our life together and our son. It's beautiful. The hallway has four doors, each of them open as we pass. The first on the left is a bathroom, but Aden doesn't stop. I catch a glimpse of a large room as we pass it on the right, and the final two doors are across from each other. We step into the one on the left and I don't think my eyes can get any bigger. A crib similar to Leo's old one sits in the middle of the room, with safari sheets to match the pale green walls and animal rugs along the floor.

Aden lays him in his crib, and Leo smiles in his sleep, as if he knows he's home. We back out of the room, and I know I'll marvel at the beauty and detail of it all tomorrow as Aden shuts the door and takes me across the hallway.

A massive bed is pushed against the wall, the four large posts have a black netted curtain tied to them, with matching silk sheets. Aden jerks me to his chest, wrapping his arms around me as his mouth crushes to mine. "Welcome home," He murmurs against my lips.

Warm tears track down my cheeks, and he pulls away to rest his forehead against mine.

"Until the day I take my last breath, this is our home, my love." He says. I shake my head and he pulls back with a confused look. I place my palm over his steadily beating heart and smile up at him.

"This is my home." I say. Aden grabs me by my thighs, lifting me up effortlessly and backing towards the bed. The backs of his legs hit the frame and he falls backwards with me straddling his lap as he tugs the zipper down my back. His hands drag down my bare back and he groans as my dress pools around my waist, showing that I'm not wearing a bra. He cups them both gently, biting at them just enough to send shivers up my spine.

Any insecurities I may feel when I look in the mirror fade when he stares at me. Regarding me as if I'm the most beautiful creature on earth. Aden rolls over, slamming my back to the bed before he stands and tugs my dress over my legs to toss it aside. I lay there as he unbuttons his shirt, watching me squirm from the cool air around my body.

He drops his shirt and slides his hands up my legs to hook his thumbs under my panties, pulling them down while kissing the inside of my thighs, making his way across both of them. His breath fans across my exposed skin, making my thighs press together from the chill but he grips my knees and forces my legs apart with a deep groan.

"You will not hide from me, my love." He pins me with a look so full of heat I can nearly feel my body melt under his gaze. Aden is still wearing his dress slacks, not hiding the obvious outline of his erection as he slowly kneels on the floor and drags me suddenly to the edge of the bed.

"I will kneel for you every morning and night if it means I get to taste you," He murmurs as he buries his face between my thighs without hesitation. His tongue flicks over my clit, making me grip the sheet when he closes his mouth over it and sucks. He plunges two fingers inside of me, curling them as he continues his torment with his mouth devouring me until I'm trembling and whimpering his name.

My orgasm crests, waves of pleasure washing over me as I cry out and my back arches off the bed. Aden hums as he leans away, making a show of licking his lips and fingers clean. I watch him through heavy lidded eyes, still catching my breath as he stands and pushes his pants to his ankles.

"You are so delicious, I could feast on you for days. But I'm not a patient man tonight and I need to be inside of you," He crawls across the bed as I drag myself backwards with a playful smile. Aden grabs my ankle and yanks me beneath him. "I told you, you're never getting away again."

"Good," I whisper, pushing myself up to kiss him. His tongue pushes past my lips and I can taste myself on him as the head of his cock presses against me. Aden isn't gentle, he thrusts forward hard and buries himself inside of me with a groan, stealing my breath.

I cling to him as he thrusts forward, again and again as kisses along my neck, sucking and biting at the tender flesh. He rolls us over so that I'm riding him, but he still lifts his hips to meet me, burying him deeper as I twist and pinch my nipples.

"Fuck Nina, you are incredible." He moans, and that sound alone shoots between my thighs where his hand slips, twisting circles around my swollen clit. I fall forward, my hands smacking to his chest as I let myself be at his mercy. Ecstasy is just beyond reach until he finds the perfect rhythm, and it pulls me over the edge. Aden keeps his pace, prolonging the pleasure until I can't take any more. He grabs my hips and continues to bounce me on him and his fingers dig in, and his movements stutter as he fills me with his release. Aden rubs his hands up my back, kissing the top of my head as I lay on his chest in bliss.

He throws the sheet over me, rolling sideways while still buried inside of me. "I don't want to move yet, just lay with me for a while?" He asks, his voice husky enough to make me shiver as I nod. We get to spend the rest of our lives here, wrapped up in our own little paradise.

Epilogue

ADEN

Jared is a mess. Markus is rocking his son, the little guy is just a few weeks old and seems so small in his father's arms. Luna is sobbing loudly in the other room while Nina and Isabelle are doing their best to help her. Jared is pacing, until a small cry has his head whipping up as he runs for the bassinet and nearly knocks me to the wall in his rush. Alec snorts, shaking his head at the new father. Leo is climbing across Amelia, giggling as she tickles him and tolerates his sticky little hands.

"Why is she so worked up again?" I ask as he lifts his daughter as if she will break if he moves too suddenly. Markus coughs to cover his laughter, considering Aurora is small enough that Jared could cradle her with one hand.

Jared sighs as he shuffles towards the rocking chair, sitting down and brushing his nose against her head of dark blonde hair. "She needed stitches, so you imagine peeing with open wounds down your dick hole and then ask me again." He grunts, brushing his finger along Aurora's pink cheek. Each of us visibly cringes, and Xavier kicks up a crying fit in Markus' arms.

"Me too, little buddy." Markus sighs, handing him to Alec as he digs through the diaper bag. He finds the pacifier, but after just a few moments, Xavier makes it clear that he isn't having any of it and starts crying loudly.

Luna shuffles out with Nina and Isabelle close behind. Nina sits a pillow on the couch, and as Luna eases down onto it, Isabelle sticks pillows on each side of her. Jared brings Aurora over and sits next to Luna, kissing her cheek with a proud smile as he gently hands their daughter to her.

I wrap my arm around Nina as I look around, struck by a wave of belonging. This is my family, our family and it's right where we belong. Together, supporting each other through anything and everything.

The End of His Paradise.

Acknowledgements

I can't believe I'm sitting here, thinking about the infinite list of people that have helped me get to this point where I can say that I have published five books. My amazing family, that I couldn't have been more blessed with.

My Aunt's and Uncles fed my love of reading with countless ebooks, paperbacks and trips to the library. My grandparents would watch me scrabble my way up my favorite tree in their yard to sit and read for hours. Mamaw would always remind me to stop reading in the dark, and send me to bed when she found me still curled up with a book at six am. Papaw would always tease me, in the most loving way, and just enjoyed seeing my happiness from whatever book my nose was buried in.

Mom got me my first library card when I was nine and sat at her computer with me for hours every day as we wrote beautiful fantasy tales of a young adventurer. Dad would always listen when I rambled on about my latest read, even if I'd already told him before.

And the day I told my husband that I have always wanted to be an author, he grabbed his keys and pushed me to the store to buy my first laptop.

And the next one, and the next one and.... I have a history of being clumsy. But he hasn't stopped being my biggest supporter. My biggest fan through it all. I love you so much, Zachary. And to our kids, (I hope you don't read anything in this book, except this page) I chased my dream to show you that you can too. May all your biggest dreams come true, my loves.

My friends, BETA reading the absolute hot mess I drop into your laps.. What would I do without you? I sincerely hope I never find out, because I owe SO MUCH to you all! I love you. Anytime I'm stuck, or need advice, you guys are here day and night. (Aly, I hope you enjoyed meeting your book boyfriend. Markus is such a charmer hahaha.)

And Danielle, you're slowly the amount of gray hairs that pop up on my head every time I even think of the word format.. I love you so much.

How did I get so lucky to have so many incredible people in my life? I will never know, but I swear to never for a moment take any of you for granted.

That includes YOU! Amazing, wonderful, and cherished reader. Thank you for taking a chance on this book, and I hope that you found a beautiful escape in His Paradise.

About the Author

Natoshia has had a fondness for writing since she was a young girl, sitting with her mother at the computer as they created fantasy worlds full of adventure in short stories. Flash forward to today, and she is still sitting far too close to the computer screen as she types away. But now her stories are a little darker, with a pinch of excitement and a touch of spice. She has written a little of everything, from brooding mafia men to the paranormal, and now the monstrous side of books. When she's not reading or writing, Natoshia is spending time with her husband and their two children, or her beloved cat Chunky. Her favorite colors are Morally Gray and Red Flags, which is reflected in every new character she writes. She hopes you find a beautiful escape within the pages of her books.

Wanna Get Social?

https://linktr.ee/natoshiabaer

More Books By This Author

Our Darling Isabelle

She spent her entire life fixing her mother's mistakes, but this one was different. What can Isabelle do when she is offered up as payment for her mother's debt? The Barone brothers aren't used to being told no and they don't have any hesitation taking what they want. And they want her. Isabelle's problems only grow when she develops feelings for these brothers, and their enemies become her own.

"Two years. Give us two years and if at the end you still want out, you leave with your debt erased." I offer. Her eyebrows raise as she thinks it over. A few tense moments pass before she gives a curt nod.

"Fine. But at the end of the two years, I'm leaving." She says firmly. The thought nearly tears my chest open, but I smile and nod, kissing her lips.

"Deal," I whispered against her mouth.

I'm a lying son of a bitch. She's never getting away from us.

Jared's Redemption

He ran from his misery the day he became an adult, but that freedom came at a cost. Trusting a crooked man shattered the person Jared had strived to become, and he vowed to spend the rest of his life paying for his mistakes. He knew that a man like him wasn't worthy of a happy ending. Until she came along.

Luna lived a life where people constantly treated her as a possession to be polished and presented. She finally saw her chance to show her family she could be more than a pawn. All she had to do was take on the bounty to kill Steffen before anyone else. Until she saw him, tall, dark, and his face caught in a scowl. Except he was ready to take the shot that would ruin all her plans. Luna only had one choice. Tackle him to the ground, crush her lips to his, and vanish into the woods with his gun. Until her obsession became too much to bear as she fell in love with the man that she spent her days watching.

What happens when the hunter becomes the prey, tracked and followed with every step?

www.ingramcontent.com/pod-product-compliance
Lightning Source LLC
Chambersburg PA
CBHW070344010826
48976CB00019B/2421